HOME MOVIES

HOME MOVIES

PAULA MARTINAC

SEAL PRESS

This book is a work of fiction. Any resemblance to real characters or events is entirely coincidental and unintentional.

Cover photograph by Patricia Ridenour
Design by Clare Conrad

Library of Congress Cataloging-in-Publication Data

Martinac, Paula, 1954–
    Home Movies / by Paula Martinac.
        p.   cm.
    ISBN 1-878067-32-X (trade pbk.) : $10.95
    1. Women authors, American—New York (N.Y.)—Fiction.
    2. Lesbians—New York (N.Y.)—Fiction.   I. Title.
    PS3563.A7298H6   1993
    813'.54—dc20   93-17841
                                                                CIP

Printed in the United States of America
First printing, September 1993
10 9 8 7 6 5 4 3 2 1

Foreign Distribution:
    In Canada: Raincoast Book Distribution, Vancouver, B.C.
    In Great Britain and Europe: Airlift Book Company, London.

The author has contributed part of the royalties from the sale of this book to the Lesbian and Gay Community Services Center, 208 West 13 Street, New York, NY 10011.

The lines from "Nineteen Hundred and Nineteen" by William Butler Yeats are reprinted with permission of Macmillan Publishing Company from *The Poems of W.B. Yeats: A New Edition,* edited by Richard J. Finneran. Copyright 1928 by Macmillan Publishing Company, renewed 1956 by Georgie Yeats.

"you shall above all things be glad and young." is reprinted from COMPLETE POEMS, 1904-1962, by E.E. Cummings, Edited by George J. Firmage, by permission of Liveright Publishing Corporation. Copyright © 1923, 1925, 1926, 1931, 1935, 1938, 1939, 1940, 1944, 1945, 1946, 1947, 1948, 1949, 1950, 1951, 1952, 1953, 1954, 1955, 1956, 1957, 1958, 1959, 1960, 1961, 1962 by E.E. Cummings. Copyright © 1961, 1963, 1966, 1967, 1968 by Marion Morehouse Cummings. Copyright © 1972, 1973, 1974, 1975, 1976, 1977, 1978, 1979, 1980, 1981, 1982, 1983, 1984, 1985, 1986, 1987, 1988, 1989, 1990, 1991 by the trustees for the E.E. Cummings Trust.

Acknowledgments

For suggestions, stories and support, thanks to my friends Jolanta Benal, Leo Blackman, Richard Burns, Barbara Goldberg, Katie Hogan, and Ken Monteiro, and especially Penny Perkins and Steven Powsner, for their meticulous reading of the manuscript. The Blair/Kraybill family provided a writer's retreat in Los Angeles where I worked on a late draft of this novel: thanks to Joan, Nancy and baby Maggie. At different times, the encouragement and generosity of numerous other people have sustained me as a writer: Nancy Blaine, Maureen Brady, Cheryl Clarke and the Conditions Collective, Terri de la Peña, Catherine Dillon, Fran Goldstein, Anne Harvey and Gayle Green, the late Gregory Kolovakos (1951–1990), Madeleine Olnek and her writing group, all the members of Prose Acts, and Suzanne Seay, to name just a few. The Lesbian and Gay Community Services Center in New York City is my home-away-from-home, and the work I have done and the people I have met there have added immeasurably to my life and writing. Finally, my special thanks to Faith Conlon, Barbara Wilson and all the women of Seal Press for their continuing belief in my work and for making the writing of lesbians accessible.

THE PEN skidded across the paper and stopped. Teresa scratched the dried ballpoint furiously over the pad, but all it did was make a hole in the paper. She peeled the sheet violently from the pad and crumpled it into a wad she chucked at the wastebasket. It bounced off the rim and onto the floor.

"Shit," she said.

What it said on the paper was simply this: *James Patrick Keenan.*

Teresa didn't bother to pick up her litter. There were other similarly crumpled pieces tossed around the wastebasket. One or two had actually fallen in. She had not gotten far on any of the sheets. She kept expecting to hear him laugh and tease, "Sweetie, you throw like a girl."

Once she had written as much as *James Patrick Keenan, beloved friend and uncle,* but after that there seemed almost nothing left to say.

"What can I do?" she had said to Tom that morning at the apartment when they returned from the hospital. She meant make coffee, sandwiches, phone calls.

Tom had enclosed her hands in his in a way he'd never done before, not in all the years that she'd known him. His hands were surprisingly warm.

"He'll need an obituary," Tom said earnestly. "I always thought I'd write it, but then, well, you know."

"Sure," Teresa said, feeling oddly flattered and apprehensive at the same time. She was a writer, but of fiction, not of reality. Could she write something that would please Tom and do justice to Jamie?

Teresa opened a desk drawer, looking for a usable pen. She found two more dried-up ones before she discovered one that actually wrote, though it skipped and clotted in an irritating way.

It was a funny desk to be sitting at, a place where she felt small and female and young, even though she was thirty-six. Tom's desk was a massive mahogany piece polished to a ruby glow. A pharmacy lamp with an amber glass shade cast a pool of golden light across it. Her own desk was a wooden plank propped up on filing cabinets.

It was so unlike her life, theirs. Two men together made a lot more money than she'd ever have. Why didn't they have better pens?

She remembered that since he'd taken an extended leave from work to care for Jamie, Tom hadn't touched the novel he'd been laboring to write in his spare time over the years. He had no more spare time. And in the two merciless years of Jamie's illness, Tom's pens had all dried up.

"I'm writing it in my head," he told her once when she inquired. It was after Jamie's second bout with PCP. Tom looked worn and lank, not all that healthy himself, and she noticed that he was smoking again, after having quit for a short time.

"The rest of it is up here," Tom continued, tapping his temple with his middle finger. "I'm telling it to Jamie in pieces. He seems to like it, and he's really able to stay objective. He's always been my true barometer, you know."

Teresa abandoned the faulty pen and uncovered the IBM Selectric next to the desk. Tom had still not bought a computer, though he used one at work. He wrote his novel long-hand, meticulously and neatly on unruled bond paper. Jamie had presented him with a Macintosh several Christmases before, but they returned it after only two weeks.

"Hurts the writing," Tom rationalized. "Makes you sloppy. It's not for my *serious* work." He was always belittling his career as a television writer, saying that scripting sophisticated cop and lawyer shows didn't count as art.

Teresa faltered at the touch of the typewriter keys, so much stiffer than those on her inexpensive computer. After another false start, she tapped out a complete sentence.

James Patrick Keenan, 56, a local gay activist, died at New York University Medical Center in Manhattan on June 1, 1990, of complications associated with AIDS.

.   .   .

SHE HAD said, "That can't be," and he had repeated it.

And after a pause she said, "But you and Tom have been together over twenty years. You should've been *safe* from this, for Christ's sake. This shouldn't be happening to you."

What she also meant but would never say was, how can you die on me?

"Tom and I haven't been completely monogamous," he admitted, propped up in his hospital bed, vulnerable but unapologetic. "I mean, twenty-four years is a long time, Teresa."

It *is* a long time, she wanted to scream. It's a lifetime. You could have had another lifetime with him, but no. It's too long to go without fucking around.

Then she stopped herself.

"We were . . . social," he continued, vaguely. "We liked variety. Tom is particularly imaginative when it comes to sex." He said it in the present tense, but in the age of AIDS she knew imagination in sex meant something altogether different than it used to.

5

She sighed. "You haven't told anyone else in the family, I guess?"

He fussed with a crease in the top sheet. "No, sweetie, you have the distinct honor of being the first."

Suddenly she felt like two halves splitting apart, ripped cleanly in two like a sheet of paper. One half was body, the other something else, emotion or essence maybe, watching as her body made movements toward Jamie, hugged him, patted his arm, rubbed his leg affectionately through the sheet. She had experienced this before. After her sister Alison died, Teresa went back to school after a month at home, a stranger to her fourth-grade classmates. Children are forgetful. Her second day back she threw up during geography class, quietly, while Miss Bryant's back was turned. Only Vivian Masetti, who sat behind her, noticed. Later, smelling the mess under her desk, Teresa didn't remember throwing up; she was completely divorced from the sensation of it. She had merely observed herself doing it, while the other part of her, the real part, was somewhere else, in one of the far-off places she'd never been but often imagined.

Her two halves reunited. "Do you want me to tell Dad?" she asked. She could face telling her father, not her mother. The last time she had mentioned AIDS at home, her mother had said, "You know, some people say AIDS is God's punishment to homosexuals."

She wanted to snap, "Some people say people like you are God's punishment to homosexuals," but she wasn't brave enough to say something she only felt at that moment, in a desire to strike back. "It's a virus, Mother," she had answered instead, "not God's wrath."

"Well," her mother finished in the way she finished many conversations, "I'm not sure about that."

"I could tell Dad," Teresa offered again. Her father was also unenlightened, but more quietly so than her mother.

"Would you?" Jamie asked, a detached look on his face. "I . . . it's a lot to ask, sweetie, I know, but my big brother . . . I can't take the morality police right now."

"I know," she said, shifting closer to him on the bed and wrapping an arm around his shoulders. His back was broad, and her arm barely stretched around. Only the tips of her fingers reached to his right shoulder. She wanted more, to enfold him, encase him in a safety net. For the first time in a long time, she recalled an image of Alison. At Christmas just months before she died, Alison rested in the big armchair in the living room next to the tree, wrapped in an old pink blanket from when she was a baby. It wasn't cold in the room, but somehow keeping Alison warm was considered important. Alison's tawny head lay despondently against the chair back, her eyes a cheerless shade of green. Teresa wasn't allowed to play with her new toys in the living room, as she had every other year, always with Alison. She had to drag them into the dining room where she wouldn't "bother" her sister. Alison sat for hours, just staring at the tree lights flickering, motionless in the old pink blanket, like a giant baby longing for the womb.

Teresa gently rippled her fingers on Jamie's shoulder. "I know," she said to him again, more softly, so she wouldn't disturb him.

. . .

FOR WEEKS after her parents took Alison to the hospital the last time, Teresa stayed with her grandmother across town and didn't have to go to school. Every few days, Miss Bryant, her teacher, brought Teresa assignments to do at home. Miss Bryant stayed and listened to Teresa read aloud from one of the books she chose from the school library.

She didn't see her mother much during that time, but her father came to visit every night. He said her mother couldn't come very often because she had to sleep in Alison's hospital room. Teresa wondered if her mother was sick, too, and her father and grandmother just weren't telling her the truth. Her queries of "Is Mommy okay?" always received a positive response, but a look passed between the two adults that Teresa worried about, a look that seemed to say more than they did.

At first, it was exciting to stay at Grandma's, and not going to school was a novelty. But after a couple of weeks, Teresa tired of it and began to wonder what Raymond Schmidt had done recently to upset Miss Bryant, and if Karen Costello's mother had had her new baby yet. She missed Valentine's Day and the pink-frosted cupcakes served in the cafeteria at lunch, but Miss Bryant brought her a card signed by the whole class, a cut-out bluebird carrying a heart reading "You Sure Are Tweet." Miss Bryant also brought more books, and they were the biggest relief for the tedium.

There were the Little House series, the Betsy books, *A Little Princess*, and Winnie the Pooh. Pooh was perfect at bedtime, when Grandma read her anything she requested. Teresa didn't always understand it, but she liked the sound of the stories, the way Grandma read the dialogue in an exaggerated English accent, and she was especially fond of Piglet. She and Grandma were well through *The House at Pooh Corner* the night that her mother and father both stopped in at Grandma's.

Her mother's mascara had run down her cheeks in dotted black lines. Her father's face was ashen as the winter sky. When they entered her room at Grandma's, Grandma cried "Oh, no!" until Teresa's father guided his mother downstairs with his arm wrapped tightly around her waist, as if she couldn't walk on her own.

Teresa's mother's body gently indented the mattress as she sat and retrieved the book Grandma had dropped on the wooden floor. Then she lay down softly beside Teresa on top of the covers.

"Is this the place?" she asked, opening to where the pages had creased in the fall to the floor. Teresa nodded yes, numbly, automatically, though it was a different spot altogether, an earlier chapter they had read two nights before.

"By the time it came to the edge of the Forest the stream had grown up," her mother read, "so that it was almost a river, and, being grown up, it did not run and jump and sparkle along as it used to do when it was younger, but moved more slowly. For it knew now where it was going, and it said to itself, 'There is no hurry. We shall get there someday.'" Her mother continued to read, her words wavering, until she had to stop because her eyes were blurred with tears.

"Teresa," she said in a watery voice, her head bent away from Teresa's on the pillow, "I have something very sad to tell you. Something very sad that's happened. Alison... Alison's passed away."

That was all she said before she exploded into sobs so resounding that Teresa's gentle patting did nothing to stop them. In fact, her attempts at comforting only seemed to make things worse. Teresa's father walked back upstairs and led her mother away, too. In a few minutes he returned and kissed Teresa's forehead.

"You try to sleep," he urged her in a whisper. He looked tired and thin, with unkempt hair his hand had set on end, sunken cheeks, and a vacant stare in his eyes. After he switched off the lamp, Teresa saw his form in the doorway, standing motionless. She dozed off but when she woke up he was still there, a silent sentry in the dark night.

By morning her father had left his post at the door of Teresa's room, the one that had once been Uncle Jamie's. Her mother and father stayed overnight at Grandma's, too, sleeping in the twin beds that had been his and Uncle Pete's. The room hadn't changed since they were teenagers, he said, which was more than twenty years. "A shrine to our boyhood," he mused. Two walls were completely covered in maps of the world, Ireland, the United States, Pennsylvania, and Pittsburgh, their entire sphere in descending order. On the map of the United States, the two boys had circled in red every city and town they'd ever visited. Western Pennsylvania was clogged with red circles, and they were also scattered throughout Ohio and West Virginia. Later, during the war, Grandma continued the practice by drawing red rings on the world map around the Philippines and Hawaii.

Sometime during the night, her mother and father had joined each other in one of the twin beds. They both looked small to Teresa as she spied on them from behind the door. She could only see the tops of their heads poking out of the layers of blankets Grandma had folded on top of them.

"You let them sleep," Grandma said from behind her, closing the door quietly. "They've had a hard night."

Grandma and Teresa padded off downstairs, Grandma in the faded striped cotton housecoat she always wore, Teresa in her soft flannel pajamas with tiny roses on them. The old floorboards ached with the restraint of their movements. Grandma set out Frosted Flakes with sliced banana, not too much milk, just the way Teresa loved it. For herself, she brewed a strong cup of Lipton tea with three sugars and lots of milk. She always let Teresa have the last sugary sip.

Grandma didn't say much. She was quiet like Teresa's father, like Teresa, someone who had to be coaxed to speak. Teresa's mother and Alison, on the other hand, were chatterboxes who never lacked for something to say.

Grandma absently added the sugar to her tea with an unusually soundless stirring. Through a big bite of cereal, Teresa asked, "What did Mommy mean, Alison passed away?"

Grandma lifted her spoon from the teacup and watched as drops of tea rolled off it back into the cup. She laid it carefully on the table with a frown, as if she didn't like the question.

"That's all your mother said?" she asked.

Teresa nodded, chasing a slice of banana around the bowl with her spoon until she trapped it.

"Teresa, Alison was very sick," her grandmother began to explain. "You know that?"

"Yeah," Teresa said, "she's got leukemia," with extra emphasis on the first syllable.

"That's right." Grandma took a small sip of tea, then added more milk to the cup. She stirred again, mesmerizing Teresa with the swirling of the spoon through the liquid. Teresa could almost taste it, the sweet, tepid tea a perfect finish to breakfast.

"There's no cure for leukemia," Grandma continued. "People with leukemia can only stay well for so long, and then they begin to slip away. Eventually they die, and God takes them up to heaven."

The word "die" leapt out at Teresa. No one had explained how sick Alison really was. Teresa had a limited experience of death. Jesus had died for the sins of the world in an awful way, nailed to a cross. President Kennedy had died last fall in Dallas, leaving behind a pretty wife and children younger than Teresa. Alison and Teresa's goldfish, Spanky and Lulu, had both died on the same day and been buried in an empty crayon box in the back yard.

She knew what it meant to be sick. Alison had been sick for a long time, as much as two years, and was always making trips to the doctor and to the hospital. Teresa had been sick a number of times herself, with measles and mumps and once with bronchitis, but she never got as much attention as Alison did. When Alison was in Pittsburgh Children's Hospital, Teresa prayed for her every night, a special prayer to God to make her better soon. At mass one Sunday, Father

Donohue asked the parish to remember Mary Alison Keenan in their prayers. All those prayers should have done some good if God was listening, which Grandma assured her he was.

"That's why Alison was in the hospital for such a long time," Grandma went on, taking another swallow of tea, which was getting close to the bottom of the cup. "Because she had started to slip away. But there wasn't much the doctors could do, she was just too sick. Then last night God said, 'I want Alison here with me so she won't be sick anymore.' And he took her away to be with him in heaven. Now we have to try to remember Alison as she was."

A picture of a healthy Alison drew itself in Teresa's mind, from a home movie her father had made the last summer the family traveled to Lake Erie and stayed at a cabin within skipping distance of the shore. Alison was nine, Teresa seven, and Alison wasn't sick yet. The cabin was a snug retreat, and Alison cavorted in front of it in a polka-dotted bathing suit that was Teresa's favorite color, cornflower blue, her mother called it. Teresa asked if their room could be painted cornflower blue, but their father had just painted it peppermint pink a few months before and pink it would stay. Alison picked the pink, she being older and more vocal about her likes and dislikes. Teresa could picture Alison in that bathing suit, her arms strong and tan, running into the water and out again to press her face close to their father's camera lens. She was always swimming, like Teresa had wished she could. But the home movie caught Teresa watching her sister cautiously from the shallow water, because she had only just learned to doggie paddle.

Teresa thought about God taking Alison away. What was Alison doing in heaven? Was she still bundled in the pink blanket, or could she run and swim again like in Daddy's movie? In religion class, they had learned that heaven was a beautiful place with no pain or suffering or want. But there was no coming back, she knew that much. Returning from death was something Mommy had assured her didn't happen, after a ghost story on television had given her nightmares. Something started squeezing Teresa's chest as she realized she would never see Alison again. She hadn't even said goodbye. All Teresa could think was "I hate you, God, for taking Alison." If she could have been face to face with God at that moment, she would have kicked him.

The sound of the empty teacup on the saucer snapped Teresa back to her grandmother's kitchen. Grandma was already whisking the cup and saucer to the sink, where she rinsed them and placed them on the counter. Grandma had never before forgotten to give her the last sip, the one where, no matter how much it was stirred, lots of sugar had settled. But it didn't matter. Teresa's tears were already dropping off her nose into her cereal bowl, mingling with the leftover milk and flakes.

.   .   .

DURING SOME of their adult relationship, Teresa and Jamie hid in different closets. Jamie didn't formally tell her he was gay until she decided to remain in New York after college and not return to Pittsburgh. He said he was waiting for her to be "old enough." For some inexplicable reason, she waited to tell him until two years after his own admission, even though at the time he came out to her she was at the start of her first relationship with a woman, a graduate student named Roz. Teresa convinced herself that she waited because she was confused and really at that time bisexual. When she finally told him, Jamie was patient with her on the surface, but underneath ran an angry current.

"Did you know about yourself when I came out to you?" he asked, warily.

Teresa nodded, just as cautiously. "I had a pretty good idea. I was involved with this woman, Roz. You met her. The one I shared the apartment with that summer after college?"

"But you let me go through that alone," he said, incredulously. "You let both of us go through that alone."

"I'm sorry," she said, lowering her eyes guiltily.

"Oh, sweetie," he said kindly, instead of continuing to reproach her. "It's okay." He slid an arm around her and tugged her to him. Unlike other men she knew, his movements were subtle and never overpowering. He seemed to recognize his own strength and to curb it.

"You know," he smiled, "I wondered about you when you came to visit with that college roommate of yours—what was her name? Lisa? Lena?"

"Liane."

"Liane. She dressed you up like a dyke, right down to the tie. Remember?"

Teresa swept the memory aside roughly. "There wasn't anything going on between us. We were just friends. I didn't even realize what she'd done, dressing me like that, that's how naive I was." She hardly ever thought about Liane Levin and was uncomfortable recalling what they had and hadn't been to each other.

Taking the hint, Jamie abandoned the subject. He gently squeezed her shoulder. "Just promise me something, sweetie. Don't keep anything big from me again. We're in this together." He didn't have to elaborate on the "this." When she came out to her parents the following Christmas, he coached her first and comforted her later.

Her parents already (probably) knew, but they weren't about to help her out. Over the years, her mother's mouth had become a fixed, straight line, her father's jaw as hard as Pittsburgh steel. Her mother had taken to attending mass at St. Sebastian's every morning and doing volunteer work there in the afternoons, typing the parish bulletin.

"The church is my one comfort," she said with a brittle smile.

"Oh, Mother," Teresa chided her, "you're only fifty years old, and you act like some ancient martyred saint. Do you have to be so melodramatic all the time?" Teresa was only twenty-five and still unable to recognize any of her mother in herself.

The moment of telling was not warm and moving but chilly and inert. Teresa ended up blurting out her secret in the middle of a supper in which no one was talking, because they knew what would happen if the silence caved in.

Her father rested his fork on his plate of half-eaten meat loaf and mashed potatoes. A man of few words, he had none at all to offer at critical moments.

Her mother said, in a way that made Teresa want to either giggle or cry, "Well, this doesn't come from *my* side of the family," the "my" bearing the weight of her anger and frustration. She pushed her plate aside, even though she had always instructed them that it was bad manners to do so. She continued to speak directly to her husband, who continued to remain speechless. "I told you it was a bad idea for her to go to New York. But no, you said, let her go to school wherever she wants. I thought she should go to Pitt, where we could keep an eye on her. I told you something like this would happen. All the way over there with your brother and his *friend*. She's always adored Jamie. We should have seen this coming."

Teresa took a deep breath that filled in the silence for a moment.

"Mom, I..."

"Leave the dishes, I'll clear them later. I just...can't right now." Her mother's eyes brimmed over, but she made an attempt at a smile that came out looking like her mouth hurt. She left the table softly and clicked the bedroom door closed behind her.

"Dad?"

He looked up finally, his eyes expressionless, as if he'd

removed himself from the table already. Teresa saw in an instant that he was no longer as handsome as he was when she was little.

Once they had been an attractive couple. Jamie used to call Teresa's mother "the dish." They had looked nice together, complementary, her father a reddish blonde, her mother with shiny black hair and a porcelain complexion—"black Irish," as Grandma described her. When Teresa was small and her parents dressed to go out dancing, they always coordinated their outfits so her father's tie or shirt matched something her mother was wearing.

After Alison got sick, they stopped having Saturday nights out, and Teresa missed the sight of them preparing for a special evening. Her mother dabbing Chantilly behind her ears and rubbing a little on Teresa's wrist. Her father pondering his tie rack, asking, "Eileen—the blue tie tonight?" and holding still while Teresa's mother adjusted his pocket handkerchief. Finally, Teresa's mother spraying her page boy into place and slithering into her best dress, a midnight blue sheath with a white satin bow on the shoulder. There was always some giggling as Teresa's father zipped her into it.

"Dad, are you speaking to me?"

He ran his tongue over his teeth behind closed lips, as if trying to dispel the bad taste of something. "Of course, I'm speaking to you," he said carefully. "I just haven't the slightest idea what to say."

Teresa smiled with relief.

"Has your uncle . . . ?"

"This has nothing at all to do with Jamie," she interrupted.

He nodded, but his brow was wrinkled with disbelief. "Because Jamie has always had . . . well, authority problems. He likes to shock people."

"I'm sure all his years with Tom haven't been for the

shock value," Teresa replied. "And I don't have authority problems."

"Well, good," he said. "Good." Then, after readjusting his silverware on the plate and refolding his napkin twice he said simply, "You were such an imaginative child."

. . .

"AND YOUR parents," Jamie grinned, "are the most unimaginative people I know."

Both Teresa and Tom chuckled. Teresa helped herself to another slice of pizza, one with lots of onions. She ate it carefully, conscious that their four eyes were fixed on her.

"I don't know," she said through a mouthful. "Dad was terrific with my school projects. We were always making things with clay—erupting volanos, maps of Argentina."

"A secret sculptor, then?" Tom suggested.

"I wouldn't go that far," Jamie said.

"Well," Teresa observed, "there's a lot of pent-up stuff in both of them."

"If you stand too close to Eileen," Jamie said, leaning into Tom, "you can hear it rumbling around inside of her."

. . .

SHE AND Tom sat together holding each other's hands in a church on the Upper West Side of Manhattan with two hundred other people. Her father came in from Pittsburgh, the last remaining Keenan brother. Uncle Pete had been dead for ten years. He collapsed of a heart attack over the steering wheel one day while starting his Olds Cutlass in the garage, where Aunt Maggie found him. Teresa's mother and Aunt Maggie didn't make the trip to New York, and neither did Maggie's children. Grandma was in a nursing home and only remembered who her children were on certain good days.

The two hundred people were mostly strangers to Teresa, and many were strangers to Tom, too. They approached Tom and said things like, "I met him at an ACT UP action in Albany," or "I heard him speak at a rally last year, and it got me off my butt." Others said, "I couldn't believe it when I heard he was in his fifties! I thought he was ten years younger!" But they hadn't seen him at the end, in his final weeks, when he resembled a wizened old man.

Tom delivered a tribute that made Teresa cry. It concluded with the W. H. Auden poem, "September 1, 1939" that Jamie loved, that Tom had introduced him to. "We must love one another or die," Tom recited, his voice cracking so slightly Teresa wondered if anyone else had noticed besides her.

Her father could not get up to say even a few words about his younger brother. "I *can't*," he whispered hoarsely, when Teresa nudged him and suggested it might help. "Why do they *do* this?" he asked in a panicked voice, probably meaning, why couldn't it be a nice, impersonal funeral? At Uncle Pete's service, the priest had fumbled a little over his last name, saying "Keene" first before catching his error and quickly extending it another syllable.

"It's therapeutic," was all she could manage to say. She was unsure if she herself could stand and take the podium, because her knees felt like they had locked.

Teresa walked stiff-legged to the front of the church, no more than fifteen feet away, wondering if everyone noticed her fear. At the podium she gripped its sides to brace herself. She had not prepared remarks, thinking that in Jamie's honor she would venture into extemporaneous speaking.

"I'm a writer at a loss for words," she began slowly, her voice wavering through the microphone, sounding big and hollow as the church's nave. "I don't have anything profound or amusing to say. On June 1 I lost both my uncle and one of my dearest friends. Jamie Keenan had a knack for taking care of people emotionally. I can't think of a time when being with him didn't make me feel special. I feel his absence

18

acutely. He made a difference in my life, and maybe in the lives of everyone in this church today. Goodbye to one of the kindest, most generous men I'll ever know. I miss you."

The "I miss you" echoed through the long nave, and Teresa listened to it and stepped down.

Later, after everyone left the apartment reception except her and her father, Teresa said to Tom, "All I keep thinking about is how the day of my sister's funeral, Jamie took me to the movies and for ice cream. That's when I met you, remember? It was one of the best things anyone ever did for me emotionally. I wish I'd told that story at the memorial today, instead of all the rambling I did."

"You didn't ramble. It was very moving, what you said." Tom picked up some plastic cups dropped by careless mourners. "What movie did you see again? The day of your sister's funeral?"

"*Mary Poppins*," she smiled.

"That's right," he smiled back. "I knew it was either that or *The Sound of Music*." He crinkled some discarded napkins into a wad in his hand. "Jamie rented it one night and sat and sang through the whole thing. He was such a kid sometimes." Tom forgot that she had been there that night, that they had in fact sung along together, but she didn't remind him.

"I think," she said instead, "we should go see a movie right now in Jamie's honor. Let's go to the Eighty-fourth Street Cineplex and just see whatever's playing. What do you say?"

For a moment something in his eyes suggested he would say no, like a rerun of the day of Alison's funeral, when Jamie hesitated before agreeing to *Mary Poppins*.

"Would your father want to come?" Tom asked finally.

"I'll ask him," she replied.

. . .

19

THE DAY of the funeral, Uncle Jamie took a day off from his real estate job and came to baby-sit.

"So, sweetie," he said, trying to feign his usual offhand air, "what should we do today?"

When she suggested that they see *Mary Poppins*, Jamie looked at her blankly, almost as if he'd forgotten who she was. Teresa was sure it meant no.

"Well, I don't know," he replied. "You know it's..." But he never finished the sentence. Instead he helped her on with her coat, right over her play clothes, and whisked her off in his sleek blue Comet, the one he drove to "pick up dates." That was a phrase Teresa's father used.

"Got to go, sweetie," Jamie would say after a visit.

"Got to go pick up your date?" her father would wink. Teresa had never seen any of the dates, but she pictured them as beautiful, dark-haired women who liked the smell of Aqua Velva and the scratch of Jamie's cheek against their own.

"We'll probably get into trouble for this," Jamie told her on the way to the movies. "But you just let me do the talking when we get home."

Like her father, Jamie was quiet, with the same soothing voice, and the silence when she was with him was companionable and not awkward. Teresa wondered if he talked more to his dates, but she wouldn't dare ask.

Jamie had nice hands, and she liked to watch him drive. His fingers were long with perfectly smooth, rounded nails, and his knuckles were faintly pink. Sometimes he only steered with one hand while he held a cigarette with the other. That day he had one hand over Teresa's on the blue vinyl car seat.

It was a weekday afternoon, and there was no crowd for *Mary Poppins*. They were early and had to wait a half hour for the show, so Jamie bought her popcorn and an orange soda pop. When Teresa accidentally smeared popcorn butter on her top, Jamie just rolled his eyes.

"Now we're in trouble for sure," he said.

"Mommy always makes me wear a dress downtown," Teresa noted, delightedly, "and she says popcorn at the show costs too much."

The movie mesmerized Teresa. Jamie didn't complain at all when she wanted to sit in the first row. With her parents, she had to sit in the middle of the theater, and with Grandma, she was forced to the back row. But her bachelor uncle, like a big, grown-up kid, liked what she liked. He slouched in his seat and stared transfixed at the screen. She spilled some orange pop, and he didn't care. She started to sing along with "A Spoonful of Sugar," and he didn't scold.

As wonderful as Jamie was, Mary Poppins was even better, and from the first row she was larger than life. She produced hat racks and wall mirrors out of her carpetbag. She had a zany chimney sweep friend and an uncle who couldn't stop laughing. She made merry-go-round horses come to life and penguins dance, and best of all, she could fly away any time she chose. And it didn't hurt a bit that she was so pretty.

The movie was over too soon. As the strains of "Let's Go Fly a Kite" faded and the theater emptied, Jamie helped her on with her coat. "Good choice, sweetie," he smiled.

"Could we see it again?" she asked, sighing.

"Not today," Jamie replied, suddenly serious and adult.

In the lobby, Jamie bought her the sound track of the movie—"So you'll know all the words next time we come"—and a copy of the book. The picture on the book's cover didn't look anything like the people in the movie, but Teresa knew she'd like it just the same, as long as it was about Mary Poppins.

Because Jamie's mood had turned somber, Teresa was surprised when he offered to buy her ice cream at Howard Johnson's. He kept glancing at his watch, aware of the time.

"If we're going to get into trouble," he reasoned, "we might as well go all the way."

She got to order a sundae instead of just a scoop of ice cream, so she chose butter pecan with butterscotch topping, whipped cream and rainbow sprinkles.

"Don't get it on your book," Jamie cautioned. "Here, let me put it over here, out of your way."

Jamie drank black coffee and smoked a cigarette. Every so often, he plucked some tobacco off his tongue with his thumb and index finger. The waitress, a girl with a bouncy ponytail, kept hovering around the table, refilling Jamie's coffee cup and smiling at him in a shy, giggly kind of way.

"She likes you," Teresa said, through a sticky mouthful of butterscotch.

He smiled nonchalantly, as if he were used to the attention, as if girls with bouncy ponytails fussed over him all the time. "You think so?" but he continued to watch Teresa eat and to ignore the waitress.

When he motioned for the check, the waitress hopped over to the table. "That's a pretty little girl you've got," she commented, looking fondly at Teresa, who now had ice cream on her top, too. "Looks just like you, with that pretty blonde hair."

"She's my niece," Jamie corrected.

"Oh, is that so?" the waitress smiled broadly. "A day out with your uncle, huh?" and she tousled Teresa's hair.

Jamie smirked at the check after the waitress disappeared.

"What?" Teresa asked.

"Nothing," he said, but Teresa plucked the check from his hand and inspected it. The waitress had written "Jeannie" and her phone number on it. A zero was in the shape of a heart. Jamie turned the bill upside down on the table with payment and tip.

"Jeannie and Jamie sittin' in a tree," Teresa teased him

22

in a sing-song voice as they left the booth, and he tickled her to make her stop.

"Come on, sweetie," he said, ushering Teresa out the glass doors. He smiled back at the waitress and said, "Thanks a lot." She called, "Any time, handsome!" after him, making Jamie blush a deep pink.

As Jamie was unlocking Teresa's side of the car, an unfamiliar voice cut across the parking lot. "Jamie?" Both Teresa and her uncle turned to spot a young man with curly brown hair and an appealing, slightly off-center smile getting out of his car not twenty feet away.

"Jamie, right?" he asked again, holding out his hand, which Jamie shook in a confused, embarrassed way. "Jamie Keenan. You don't remember me. Tom Snow. We met a month ago at Bar None. I'm a friend of Harry Wilkeson."

"Oh, sure, right, of course. You're the writer," Jamie smiled shyly.

"Well, I don't know if I'm *the* writer, but I'm flattered you think so," Tom continued, glancing at Teresa with surprise. "And who's this?"

"My niece, Teresa," Jamie answered, with a hand firmly on her shoulder. Teresa felt his grip tighten a little. "We've just been to see *Mary Poppins*."

Tom gave Jamie another big smile. "No kidding. Is that what's been keeping you busy? I haven't seen you since that night at the bar. I asked around, but none of the guys had."

"My niece—my other niece—was very sick," Jamie replied, and Teresa suddenly remembered Alison. She'd forgotten that Alison wouldn't be at home to talk to when they got back. She would have liked *Mary Poppins*, particularly the part where the penguin waiters brought raspberry ice for Mary, Bert and the children.

"I hope she's okay," Tom said.

"Well...thanks," Jamie answered quickly, his face blanching. "Look, we have to get going, Teresa'll be late for supper, but . . . why don't I give you a call?"

Tom fumbled for a pen, but the only thing they could find to write on was Jamie's arm. Tom held it gently as he inked the numbers onto Jamie's wrist, under the cuff of his jacket.

"Don't go and wash it off," Tom smiled. "But if you do, I'm in the book." Tom gave Teresa a little wave, a coy ripple of his fingers in the air, and strode off toward the restaurant.

Jamie was even more quiet on the way home. Teresa clutched her record album and book and listened to the radio that he had turned on low. She tried to sing along with "Dominique," but all she knew was "Dominique, -nique, -nique" because the rest of the song was in French. Instead, she made up words in a nonsense language, which made Jamie smile.

"Remember," he reminded her, "let me do the talking when we get home. Oh, and there's no need to mention running into Tom Snow."

He didn't say why, and she didn't ask.

. . .

Uncle Pete arrived one evening after work to take away Alison's bed for his little daughter Beth, who had outgrown her crib. "Turn it to the right, Rich . . . that's it . . . you've got it," Uncle Pete directed Teresa's father as they maneuvered the box springs through the narrow doorway. Teresa had to stay out of their way, so she struggled to concentrate on her arithmetic homework at the kitchen table while her mother washed the dinner dishes. She could hear the grunts and groans of the men as the bed left the house piece by piece, mattress, box springs, frame. Her mother clattered the dishes more loudly than usual, and—just as Teresa pondered the solution to 32×15—let a glass slip to the kitchen floor. It shattered resoundingly, several shards shooting clear across the room to Teresa's feet.

"Don't move," her mother said worriedly, noting that Teresa was in her stocking feet. "Just don't move an inch." She stared at the shattered glass in a confused way before picking up the whisk broom and dustpan and busily sweeping up the mess.

Teresa's mother had to crawl under the kitchen table to reach the pieces that had flown toward Teresa. Teresa ducked her head so she could watch. Her mother's face was strange and twisted and within seconds, tears ran down both cheeks.

"Mommy," Teresa said, climbing off the chair and down to the floor where her mother was kneeling and crying. "Mommy, get up. It's okay." It frightened her to see her mother on all fours like that under the kitchen table, like a whimpering animal. Teresa tugged at her arm and repeated "Mommy, get up," until she was heard. Her mother stared at her in surprise, as if she wasn't sure how either of them had ended up in that position. She started to stand up, hit her head, and her tears dissolved into laughter.

"Now isn't this silly," her mother said, inching out more carefully and straightening up. "It's like. . . . " She didn't say what it was like, but Teresa was reminded of something. When they were much smaller, Teresa and Alison used to pretend the table was their cave and they were mining for gold. Teresa hadn't been under the table in years, and memories of the cave game came flooding back. Like all their games, it had been Alison's invention.

"There's some gold over there." Alison pointed toward the far corner. "You crawl over and dig it out, while I work here." Teresa followed orders, but the small distance between them—perhaps one foot—seemed like an enormous chasm. She chipped away at the imaginary gold and slid back to Alison's side as quickly as she could.

"Good job. This makes one thousand dollars." Alison grinned, stuffing the make-believe lump of gold into the pocket of her overalls. Teresa beamed with pride. "Pretty soon we'll be rich enough so that Daddy won't have to work anymore."

"And we can buy a big house," Teresa chimed in.

"With a maid for Mommy."

"Daddy can get a new car."

"We could have a horse."

"And that red bike in the window at Collier's."

There was a hand on her arm, pulling at her insistently. "Teresa, come out from under there now." Her mother was still smiling, but it was a fragile smile that looked like it could break at any moment. "I'd like to have a picture of how silly we looked under there." Teresa stood up and found herself enveloped by her mother's arms, her face pressed oddly to her breasts, then released just as abruptly. She wouldn't have minded staying that way, her mother hadn't held her in a while, but the moment was quickly over.

Her mother spoke haltingly. "Let's not . . . there's no need to tell Daddy about the glass, okay?"

Teresa nodded reluctantly. The scene her father had missed seemed worth mentioning to him, but she was accustomed to the idea that some things just weren't talked about. This time she felt like her mother had let her in on a secret. Teresa returned to her multiplication problem and was just taking five times two and carrying the one, when her father appeared in the kitchen door frame.

"Done," was all he said.

. . .

ROBIN LEFT her on a Tuesday, and after that Teresa was celibate for over two years. At first it was unintentional, but as months rolled along, it became a conscious choice not to have anyone in her bed. It made her feel more in control of her life. A number of women tried to coax her into sex or marriage, but they were all wrong. Among them: the paralegal who on their second date started talking about "us" and planning a vacation together; the first-grade teacher who yearned to cook dinner for her several nights a week, her favorite meals, and sew on all her loose buttons; the graphic designer who bragged about her lavender sex toy collection; the fundraiser she probably could have been with, if she'd just had more time to get to know her. But women had a way of wanting things settled up by the second date, the sex out of the way and the road to happy merging stretching out ahead of them.

And none of them came to her readings.

It was one thing she particularly missed about Robin, her face always there in a front seat, no matter how small or insignificant the reading. Robin had heard her fiction so many times she knew parts of it by heart and sometimes used snatches of it in conversation.

When she left Robin said, "I don't know how to do this but to come right out with it—I think it's time to change our relationship."

It was not a line from Teresa's fiction.

"To what?"

"To a friendship. A platonic friendship."

Things happen. People fall in love with other people unexpectedly for reasons they can't explain. "It was a Friday." "He smiled a certain way." "She looked so vulnerable." "It was the way she asked for directions."

Robin said, "We had lunch together, and well . . . "

Yes, well.

Sometimes she looked at Jamie and Tom and the envy backed up in her like a bad meal. She'd never had a relationship that lasted more than two years. Some of her lesbian friends had been together five, six years, but their relationships were unappealing to her. Constantly together, many suffered from overzealous merging. They completed each other's sentences, got the same haircuts, assumed the same vocal intonations, checked in with each other a dozen times a day, made no individual plans. And often stopped having sex. Though she and Robin had promised at the outset that they wouldn't lose themselves in each other, it had happened anyway.

Tom and Jamie hadn't merged, even in over twenty years together. They didn't look alike, they didn't sound alike, they didn't even spend all that much time together, except on weekends. Two men together, she reasoned, were very different from two women together. That could be both good and bad. Good, because they maintained their identities. Bad, because sometimes men suppressed their feelings. Two men suppressing their feelings at the same time had to be a nightmare.

But outside their relationship, looking in, it was one that appealed to her in a certain way. When not at the television studio, Tom spent a large portion of his time alone, laboring over his novel. Jamie, the activist, founded groups, donated his time to gay organizations, gave speeches, had marathon dinner meetings. Their lives intersected in a big, rambling apartment in a venerable building on Manhattan's Upper West Side, bought for a song in the early seventies when Tom landed his first prime-time television job. Summers, it was a small house in Fire Island Pines, a brisk walk to the beach. It was a life she knew she would never have, no matter how quickly or well she wrote. There was something about the roll of the dice, the shuffle of the deck. Her hand just missed the flush by one card.

· · ·

ROBIN LEFT on a Tuesday, and on Saturday, they piled into Jamie's silver Toyota and drove aimlessly out of the city. Saturdays were sacrosanct to Jamie and Tom. It was the one day Tom didn't write anything, the one day Jamie shunned all public events and meetings. Often, it was too inviolable for even Teresa to break through, but when Robin left they made an exception.

"We're taking you away," Jamie announced dramatically on the phone. She imagined him gesturing the "away" part with a big sweeping wave of his arm. Jamie had once been so reserved, but the more public appearances he made, the more theatrical he became, as if he had wanted to be an actor all along but just overshot the turn. Teresa loved to hear him speak to an audience. He used only sketchy notes, and though he had carefully considered what he was going to say, he never memorized lines either.

"How do you do it?" she asked the first time she heard him at an AIDS rally. The writer in Teresa was uncomfortable with spoken words; they felt to her somehow misplaced.

"Oh, I sort of turn on a switch," Jamie smiled. "It's like automatic pilot."

"But it never sounds that way," she insisted. "You never say the same thing twice. You know, like Pam Brewer, who hooks onto one or two good speeches and then delivers them at every public event all year long, no matter what the occasion?"

Jamie shrugged, and she could tell he honestly didn't know where the talent came from.

"Away" meant different things to all of them, depending on what they were in the mood for. Tom thought it meant the beach. Teresa took it to mean some place north of the city, Bear Mountain maybe, or further upstate. Jamie, the driver, meant the unbroken line of shopping malls along Route 17 in New Jersey.

"What can I say? I'm from the suburbs," he grinned behind the wheel.

"So are we," Tom pointed out, "but we've overcome it."

They compromised and drove to Tom's favorite diner, Pal's, on the New York–New Jersey border, past the shopping strips and within flirting distance of the countryside.

"This is just what I needed," Teresa said, falling into the booth at Pal's. "You two take very good care of me."

"Our pleasure," Tom said, sliding in beside her.

It was enjoyable to be with them, two pleasant middle-aged men with casual charm and unconventional good looks. Jamie's hair was still fine and honey-colored, though it had thinned and receded. He had an intricate network of laugh lines around his eyes that Teresa envied. "Character lines," she called them and had started to look for them in her own face.

Tom's dark hair had grayed to salt-and-pepper, and his body was much looser than it used to be, fleshier and less compact. He still, however, got offers from young men.

"Our new script supervisor is such a hump," he announced in the car on the drive up. "He flirts with me outrageously. I told him I was married, probably for longer than he'd been on earth, and you know what he said? He said, 'I bet you're not *that* married.'"

Tom's leg brushed against hers in the booth and rested there, and she suddenly felt very vulnerable. She remembered, as she had been trying not to, that Robin had left. In just four days time, she missed the physical contact of having a lover, she missed the dailiness of being touched. Slowly, she pulled her knee back from his, so slowly he didn't notice. He was in the middle of considering his breakfast options.

"Pancakes with strawberries? Do you think they're fresh? No, *waffles*. I'm craving fat," Tom said.

Jamie was unamused. "Look, your cholesterol is two-fifty, you haven't done a sit-up in years—how about the granola and yogurt special?"

"I'd rather die," Tom rejoined.

"Well, the way you're going at it, you just might," Jamie snapped.

"What's with you, Miss Bitch? I'm supposed to have granola while you low-cholesterol types order French toast? Why did we come here anyway, if not to have a *real* breakfast?"

Jamie shook his head. Teresa had never seen them stay testy for long, and the moment quickly passed. She wondered if they ever seriously quarreled and what pushed their buttons.

"Two eggs, sunnyside up, home fries, and whole wheat toast," Jamie ordered. "Do they have the heat on in here, or is it just me?" He yanked at the neck of his polo shirt uncomfortably while Tom and Teresa ordered waffles.

"I've been thinking about what's-her-name," Jamie announced, playing with his spoon.

Teresa smiled. "Robin," she said.

"Yeah, her. You know, I never liked her all that much, even though her politics are pretty good. I thought you could do much better. I mean, falling in love over lunch? Please."

"She does that," Teresa explained, wondering why she so automatically defended her. "I should have seen it coming. She fell in love with me over dessert."

"Now dessert," Jamie said, "*that* I can see. Dessert is very sexy. It's rich and luxurious, and it means it's almost time for bed. But lunch? Obviously, she's lost her style. Lunch is so . . . pedestrian."

"What was the dessert?" Tom asked. He always asked specific questions, tucking the answers into some mental file. Sometimes they showed up on prime-time television. "Do you remember?"

"It was at Yaffa Cafe, and I always have mud pie there," Teresa remembered. "And Robin probably had cheesecake. That's her favorite."

"Mud pie, there's a sexy dessert," Jamie shivered. "It makes the hairs on the back of my little Catholic neck stand up just thinking about it."

31

"Yeah, it is a sexy dessert," Teresa agreed, though she wasn't sure she liked it that the conversation had turned to sex. With Jamie and Tom, it often did.

"Anyway," Jamie continued, "you'll do better next time. We live and learn. Maybe Tom and I should have first approval."

He was trying to be light, but she felt very heavy. His charming banter, usually so appealing, just made her quiet. It was Tom who noticed.

"Enough about what's-her-name. See, we can't even remember her name! Let's talk about...waffles!" They arrived as he spoke, and breakfast broke everyone's train of thought. When they stopped passing the syrup, Tom said kindly, "Why don't you come to the Island this summer for a couple of weeks? You've never stayed more than a long weekend, and it's heavenly during the week. We'll have a regular boy-girl writers' colony. We'll pretend we're Tennessee Williams and Carson McCullers at Yaddo. Can you take two weeks?"

She smiled. She could take two weeks, but she found it unfair that she still had to work full time, even though she'd had two novels published by a women's press. Gay male writers commanded large advances and enviable contracts from big publishing houses, but few lesbians did. Tom made six figures writing for television, while she earned a fraction of his salary as a copy editor for a magazine that would never consider reviewing books with lesbian content.

"Sure," was what she said, graciously, keeping her frustration private. "That would be terrific."

"You can keep me company while Jamie's off fighting injustice and oppression."

"Someone's got to," Jamie replied, eating less of his breakfast than was normal. He pushed the home fries around his plate. "Could we get out of here? It's too goddamn stuffy."

After breakfast, they all decided they needed something from the Super Gap on Route 17, so Jamie pulled into the lot, crowded with New York license plates. Tom and Teresa were already out of their doors, discussing the merits of Gap Easy Fit jeans over Levi's 501s—"for all the baby boomers who've spread through the middle," Tom suggested. Jamie remained behind the wheel, his hands grasping it as if to hold himself up.

Tom looked back through the passenger window at him, interrupting something Teresa was saying. He walked to the driver's side and knocked at the window. Jamie was staring straight ahead, and his knuckles on the wheel were white.

"Jamie? Honey?"

After a few long seconds, Jamie turned to the window and rolled it down.

"I don't feel so great," he explained. "I feel really warm."

Tom pressed a hand to Jamie's forehead, and his face betrayed his concern. "Teresa, get back in the car," he ordered abruptly. Then he softened his tone. "Jamie's burning up. We should get him into bed right away."

Tom drove them back to the city in silence, with Teresa in front and Jamie reclined on the back seat. Tom didn't like to drive and didn't do it often. He was much more cautious a driver than Jamie, never topping fifty miles an hour.

Tom took Jamie to the hospital in the middle of the night, when his temperature rocketed to a hundred and four. That was just the beginning.

. . .

THE FIRST time Teresa heard Jamie speak in public, she thought she was listening to someone else, not her soft-spoken uncle. Robin convinced her to attend the forum.

"We've all got to do something," Robin insisted. "This idea that AIDS doesn't affect lesbians or isn't their business makes me furious. It's a larger issue. You should hear Jamie talk about it. He's a great example of someone who got off his butt late and got politicized by the epidemic."

It wasn't that Teresa didn't consider AIDS her business. She had tried to get involved politically on various issues, but then got lazy. She had stuffed envelopes for McGovern and for Mondale. Her girlfriend Dana had pushed her to abortion rights rallies and Take Back the Night marches. Robin, an ardent member of ACT UP almost since its inception, had coaxed her to a few meetings, which Teresa found overwhelming in their hugeness. It was hard to imagine where she would fit in. Other friends had cajoled her into donating time to more lesbian and gay organizations than she could count. She thought she must have been to one meeting of practically every group in the city. What she really wanted to do was stay home and write.

"You can't write in a vacuum," Robin chided. "You have to know what's going on out there. You have to take part, be a witness."

For some reason, Jamie didn't pressure her. He didn't pressure Tom. Maybe it was part of his life that he wanted to keep separate. Tom, in fact, had never heard Jamie speak publicly either. The evening Robin persuaded them both to attend an AIDS forum at the Community Center where Jamie was a guest speaker, Jamie was visibly nervous.

"Don't sit up front," he cautioned them, flexing the index cards on which he kept his brief notes, an outline so meager it made no sense to anyone else. "I'll lose my train of thought. I'll be trying to read what's going on in your heads."

They sat to the side in the back of the room, an ancient high school auditorium, trying to blend in with the mostly tee-shirted, blue-jeaned white men. Every few rows there was a white woman or a person of color. Arriving late, Robin stood in back near the Coke machine with a small band of male friends. Her whistles and hollers as Jamie introduced himself were the loudest in the room.

As he continued, the cheers died down. Teresa found herself focusing more on his style than on his words, but every so often the content of his speech jumped out at her.

"We forget," Jamie gently rebuked the audience, "that AIDS is not just a gay male issue. AIDS has struck men, women, and children, people of all colors and sexual orientations."

"But we're the hardest hit!" a faceless heckler called.

"And while it is true that the gay male population has been ravaged, hit in disproportionate numbers, it's important to guard against the tendency to see only our own suffering. I was stunned the other day to hear a friend of mine, a white gay man, claim that gay men are the most hated of all minorities. Why can't we avoid ranking our losses and oppression over those of others, and see our privilege for what it is?"

Teresa tried to determine where the few hisses were coming from, but the space was packed and columns blocked her view. Her eyes fell onto the folding chair in front of her, which had a sticker on the back of it that said "Women Wrestlers Club." Next to it another chair read "Men of All Colors Together."

"It's wrong to view the disease or ourselves in isolation," Jamie continued, eyes on his index cards to maintain his composure. "AIDS is about the oppression of all people. It's about the failure of this administration on all levels."

Cheers.

As Jamie's speech pressed on, Teresa scanned the faces around her for reactions to it. A young man to her right with a shaved head sported a leather jacket with a cock ring in the epaulet and a look of soft rapture that didn't match his tough exterior. He never took his dreamy eyes from Jamie. Did men fall in love with him all the time, she wondered, just hearing him speak? He was old enough to be a father to most of them, and his button-down style was not the fashion of this crowd. Yet the men surrounding her sat rapt and attentive, as if Jamie's words alone might hold a key to combating the horror all around them.

Cheers again, for what she wasn't sure, and Teresa realized that the speech was winding down.

"'We must love one another or die,' Auden wrote. Those are our choices. We must not die."

More cheers, more clapping, some tentative, some rigorous. Robin put two fingers into her mouth and whistled.

"Your uncle," she said excitedly to Teresa, "is a pistol."

After Jamie spoke, Tom left to have a cigarette on the sidewalk outside the building, where a small group of smokers had congregated. Teresa followed him and for maybe the tenth time in her life, she smoked, too.

They could see their breath in the fall night air. Tom was wearing only a thin denim jacket and he shivered perceptibly.

"Well," he said after a long, relieved drag.

"You were nervous for him," she observed. "Me too."

"Somebody started to hiss," he said, examining his cigarette. "I couldn't understand it. He seemed so. . . ." He stopped and looked off toward Seventh Avenue, distracted by loud honking.

"Vulnerable," she finished.

"No," he disagreed quickly, shaking his head and giving her a thoughtful look. "No, never that. I was going to say, he seemed so right."

She smiled and stamped out her cigarette in the street.

• • •

ON HER first night with Robin they never went to sleep.

Robin refused to use the euphemism "sleep with." In the middle of dessert she grabbed Teresa's hands across the res-

36

taurant table, smearing moist crumbs of mud pie on her white sleeve in an unromantic way.

"Your sleeve," Teresa pointed out, smiling at her fondly.

"What?" Robin said distractedly, looking down at the smudge of chocolate on her cuff. "Oh, fuck it, who cares? I want to have sex with you."

No one had ever said it to her so boldly or emphatically. People didn't use the word "sex" like that, they were much too genteel. Teresa had heard and used all the standard substitutions: "I want to make love with you." "I want to sleep with you." "Let's go to bed." Robin's undisguised desires made the others seem almost silly.

They had sex and talked, talked and had sex, until daylight. Once Teresa began to doze in Robin's arms but then felt Robin's lips on hers again, insistently pulling her back from sleep.

"I want to know everything about you," Robin said greedily. She was as relentless at conversation as she was at sex. "Tell me when you started writing."

It was a question Teresa was used to answering at readings and interviews, ever since her first novel was published. She always said, "I started writing at nine, to keep myself busy," but never added why she needed to keep busy.

"Were you lonely as a child?" an interviewer who wanted a longer article might ask.

"Yes," Teresa might venture, the ground under her answer feeling a little shaky. "I had a sister who died."

"I had a sister who died," she told Robin, whose eyes never left hers. "She was eleven and I was nine. She had leukemia. I used to make up stories to help her go to sleep."

Robin's deep breath filled the room. She propped herself up on an elbow, her heavy breasts dangling to the futon. Teresa expected her to say what everyone said, what never made any sense. "Oh, I'm sorry." For what? For something that happened more than twenty years before? Then Teresa was forced to say, "It's all right, really," almost comforting the other person. But it had never been all right really, not from the moment her mother told her, "Alison has passed away." There was never anything right about it at all.

But Robin was silent. She hadn't uttered the "I'm sorry" that rushed to everyone's mouth. In the dark, her lips opened and closed noiselessly, then were suddenly and inexplicably on Teresa's again.

．　．　．

THE NIGHT before Uncle Pete came to take away Alison's bed, Teresa lay watching it in the darkness of the room. She could see only the flat outline of it, where once Alison's long body had been tucked up under the covers as she whispered to Teresa in the minutes before sleep.

"Know what Brian Rooney did to Mary Ann Giannini at recess today?"

"If you promise not to squeal to Mommy, I'll tell you a new word I learned."

Teresa closed her eyes tight and pictured Alison. She recalled the first night Alison's crying in bed had woken her up, the smothered sobs escaping from under the blankets.

"Alison?"

There was silence, then Alison muttered from her corner of the room, "Go back to sleep, Trees, it's okay." Alison had always called her "Trees," for as long as she could remember. No one else did. Their mother said it was because Alison slurred the name "Teresa" when she was little. Teresa rolled over to go back to sleep, but within minutes heard more muffled crying from Alison's direction.

It was cold and she didn't want to leave her own cozy bed, but Teresa slipped out of her blankets and tiptoed over to Alison. Alison's back rose and fell with her labored breathing.

"Alison?" she said, laying a small hand on her sister's

back, trying to restrain the worrisome heaving of it. "Are you sick?" Alison didn't answer. Shivering, Teresa crawled under the covers with her, pushing Alison gently toward the wall, and pressed up close to her.

Alison's sobs became drier and harder. They felt like Teresa's own, as her body rocked with her sister's. Alison blurted out, "I hate doctors. I hate being sick." Several long minutes passed with only Alison's crying to fill them. Finally, Teresa started whispering into her sister's neck, talking gently to the fuzzy hairs that grew like soft down there.

"Want to hear something? About that beat-up old house over on Lori LaRouche's street?"

Alison seemed to nod, her crying dissipating into sniffles.

"There's a girl who lives there who doesn't go to St. Sebastian's. I've seen her when I go with Mommy to the A&P. She goes to *public* school," Teresa related, with obvious disapproval. They didn't know any children who went to public school, and certainly wouldn't have been allowed to play with them if they weren't Catholic. "Her name is Carla."

Alison's breathing slowed and became normal. She wiped her nose on the sleeve of her flannel pajamas.

"Carla what?" she asked.

"Carla Carlotta," Teresa answered, not missing a beat.

"That's a stupid name. You made it up," Alison said.

"No, I didn't, honest," Teresa insisted. "Cross my heart and hope to die."

"Don't say that," Alison hissed. "It's bad luck. Okay, go ahead with the story."

They lay together for more long minutes, with Teresa's arm draped over Alison's waist and her voice droning on in the dark. The story became more elaborate than Teresa had imagined when she started out, and she wondered herself where it would end. At last, Carla, an orphan raised by her grandmother in the ramshackle house, was discovered by a rich uncle in England and went to live with him in his castle.

"What kind of castle?" Alison asked, but she was already half-asleep, and Teresa's eyes were struggling to stay open. Alison and Teresa both liked stories about castles.

"Tomorrow night," she sighed, "I'll tell you about the castle."

That was the first of many nights of stories.

Teresa's eyes opened, and Alison still was not there. She rolled toward the wall and examined the shadows from the window that played on it. She held her hand out of the covers to make a duck shadow, but there was not enough moonlight. Finally, she whispered into her pillow.

"Alison? Want to hear something?" The stillness pressed in on her, and she tucked her head under the sheet and blanket and continued talking.

"Yesterday there was a man at Curly's, buying cigarettes. He was wearing a brown raincoat and a big black hat and his voice was scratchy, like this: 'Hey, Curly, gimme a pack of cigarettes.' You couldn't see his eyes under the hat, and he had his hands shoved into his pockets. Curly was waiting on Carla, but he ran right over and said, 'Yes, sir, Mr. Stash,' and dropped the cigarettes like he was scared."

Her voice filled the space under the blankets and sounded deep and mellow, like someone else's. She got no further than the cigarette pack fumbled by a nervous candy store owner before she lost herself to sleep.

· · ·

"I'VE BEEN worrying," Tom said over the phone, "what to do about his ashes."

Teresa was surprised, because it was the sort of thing Jamie had helped friends to plan. "You never talked about it?" she asked incredulously.

"Well, when he first found out, he talked about wanting

to make a political statement with his death, like having us throw his body on the White House lawn or something equally awful. I said I couldn't do that. So then we talked about a memorial service and that he should be cremated, no matter what his Catholic family said. We talked about the ashes kind of, well, flippantly. Just to deal with it, I guess. But I couldn't ask him seriously for a decision. I didn't know how to say it. Funny, isn't it? I've written lines for characters like that—'Scatter my ashes over Manhattan, darling.' I'd know exactly what to do if my life were a TV show and not, well, life."

In an odd way, she understood him. Her own characters' lives were always easier than her own. If she didn't like the way they were turning out, her computer had a handy delete key. Having to think about Jamie as ashes was not something she could make disappear.

"What would he like?" she asked helpfully.

For the last six months of Jamie's life and through to the memorial service a month later, she and Tom were constant companions. She lost touch with other friends, whose lack of connection to Jamie made them seem oddly dispensable. Some repeatedly left messages on her answering machine. "You think you could return one of my calls?" was the last peeved one from Gloria Rosa.

With Tom it was a progression of friendship and closeness that felt entirely normal to her, though she had spent very little time alone with him prior to that. Before, Jamie was always around, the link between them. When it was all over, when they'd sent Jamie off in style, when they'd strewn his ashes in some meaningful place, what would be left for the two of them? She worried that Tom would drift out of her life as casually as he had drifted in one day in a parking lot in Pittsburgh. And that would mean that Jamie was really gone.

"There's the beach, but he was never as big a beach per-

41

son as I am," Tom noted. "When I die, Teresa, it's definitely the beach for me."

She was so still she might have stopped breathing.

"Teresa?" Tom said softly. "I'm sorry. I'm fine, really I am. It's just that I'm fifteen years older than you, women live longer than men, it's a fact, I'm sure I'll go first, that's all. Are you still there?"

"Yes, I heard you," she replied. "The beach for you. I'll remember."

"So not the beach for Jamie," Tom continued calmly. "Maybe—well, what do *you* think?"

She carried many pictures of Jamie in her head. One was his official side, addressing groups of activists in his jeans, button-down shirts, and ACTION = LIFE button, his elegant hands sweeping the air around him as he spoke. One was his uncle persona, and in that one, he never looked older than thirty. He was the shy, slender young man who escorted her to the movies and ate as much popcorn as she did. Another more recent image was of him in a hospital bed, tired and emaciated, his IV unit emphasizing his fragility. She was afraid to stand too close to it, for fear of cutting off his lifeline. She always kept to the other side of the bed just to be sure.

"What would he like?" Tom asked. Did he realize it was the same question she'd asked him just moments before? Why couldn't the two people who were closest to him come up with any answers? They were like lost travelers rambling in circles back to their point of origin.

"Let's think," she said, stalling for time.

The silence was long and complicated, and after several seconds, Tom broke it. "Well, we're getting nowhere fast," he concluded. "Let's think it over and talk again soon."

"Tom, are you... all right?" she asked abruptly, reluctant to let him off the phone. "I mean, do you want me to come over later?" She hated asking, would rather have been invited. Her mother trained her not to ask directly for what she wanted.

"Don't insert yourself into people's lives," her mother warned. "Wait to be invited." Where did that come from? Teresa suspected it was some narrow Catholic view of the virtue of self-denial, the idea that pleasure is something you can't seek or expect.

"I'm okay," Tom said, and her heart sank an inch or two. He didn't need her, didn't care if she needed him. Then, as if reading her thoughts, he added, "But it would be nice to see you."

"Okay," she said, her spirits raised, "I'll come."

· · ·

THE TWO weeks at the beach house with Tom never materialized. Instead, Jamie got sick and spent most of the summer being shunted back and forth to doctors. He and Tom managed to escape to Fire Island for a few weeks in August, and there was an unspoken understanding that Teresa would not be joining them. Instead, she spent one week visiting friends in the Catskills and took another as single days broken over the course of a month. It did not feel like a real vacation, but then nothing felt very real that summer.

At the Gay Pride March in June, she walked with friends in the women's contingent. "Two, four, six, eight/How do you know your wife is straight?" they chanted at the spectators in the windows of the Plaza Hotel on Central Park South, men in suits with jowls, women with stiff hair. The march was fun for a while, reading the tee-shirts of the women around her. "Lesbians Are Natural Leaders—You're Following One." "How Dare You Assume I'm Straight!" "I Got This Way from Kissin' Girls." Then Teresa almost tripped over Robin and her new girlfriend carrying placards for the Lesbian Herstory Archives. Robin's was a giant photo of Eleanor Roosevelt, but Teresa couldn't look at either the

43

girlfriend or her placard. Out of the corner of her eye, she just saw a mop of dark hair. Robin said, "Oh, Teresa," in a confused way, as if seeing an ex at a pride march was somehow extraordinary. Teresa started to say "Hi," then swallowed it back. She turned to her friend Gloria, who was shouting "Hey hey, ho ho, homophobia has got to go!" and asked urgently, "Can we move back?" Spotting Robin, Gloria said immediately, "Sure, let's go."

They wandered back to where the Community Center float was blasting "I Am What I Am" while men in spandex shorts danced in formation down Fifth Avenue waving brightly colored pom-poms. Even in the crush of scantily-clad male bodies, Teresa felt like she could breathe again. Seeing Robin, her heart had pounded its way right up into her throat.

On the sidelines in crowded Greenwich Village, where the parade narrowed to almost single file, Jamie called out to her. "Sweetie!" she heard clearly above the roar of the disco music. He'd lost a few pounds in the short time since she'd seen him, and Tom had an arm wrapped protectively around his waist. Teresa couldn't reach him over the police barricades.

"I'll pull out and join you," she called past the head of a drag queen decked out like Whitney Houston. "We'll have a drink or something."

"No, don't," Jamie said earnestly, hurting her feelings a little. In the initial stages of his illness, he distanced himself from her, perhaps intentionally, until she eventually cited him for it. "You walk the rest of the way for me," he added with a smile. She smiled then, too, unable or unwilling to stay annoyed or hurt for long. It wasn't worth it, she thought, especially not now.

At the Christopher Street Fair at the end of the march she wandered away from Gloria and her other friends, consciously trying to get lost. She suddenly needed to be alone and knew Gloria would try to talk her out of it. As she turned to make her way up Hudson, away from the crowds on Christopher, she caught sight of Gloria holding a bottle of Budweiser, looking back and forth, obviously concerned at having lost Teresa. Stealthily, Teresa cut her way through the cramped Village streets and home to her walk-up in Chelsea. The familiar sight of the building filled her with relief—the gray paint peeling off the bricks, the latticed black fire escape with a cat loose on it, the geraniums like red and white banners in her neighbor's window, welcoming her home. She could think of nothing but the solitude and comfort of her little apartment.

She was alone the entire evening, ordering in pizza and camping out on her old sofa, the one Tom and Jamie had given her when they purchased leather. With the lights off, she watched a rerun of *Murder, She Wrote* and a badly scripted made-for-TV movie about child abuse. The answering machine picked up her calls, two from Gloria, one from another friend, none from Jamie, none from Robin.

At ten o'clock she considered trying to hook up with Gloria again. In one of her messages Gloria had left the address of the party she and the others had gone to. But it was clear across town in the East Village, too close to Robin's apartment, and Teresa found she couldn't pry herself from the room. Instead, she sat at her desk, drew out a spiral notebook where she accumulated story ideas, and jotted a few notes onto a clean sheet.

"Fifth Avenue, New York City. Use gay march somehow as a motif for the decline of a relationship. They're together at one, apart for one, with different people at a third. Too hokey?"

Writing the words "with different people" gave her an odd, buoyant feeling that urged her out onto the fire escape to watch the moon, the brightest disk of white gold she had seen in a long time.

. . .

Teresa was working on her third novel, but she was stuck. She sat at her desk for many light summer mornings before going to work and stared out the window at the row of buildings across West Fifteenth Street. In a fourth-floor window just catty-corner, a white woman in a shimmery blue kimono posed most mornings having coffee. If she knew Teresa was watching, she didn't let on. She drank her coffee in sips so tiny maybe they weren't real at all. Maybe, Teresa thought, everything was an affectation—the coffee, the way the kimono dropped off her shoulder, the way she tugged it closer to her breasts, which were small and rounded. Maybe she was putting on a show for someone in a window on Teresa's side of the street, maybe Teresa, more likely a man.

Teresa had never been stuck in her writing for so long. There were occasional dry spells and days when everything she wrote resembled cardboard. The bad days. But it had now been a month of bad days, one following the next in quick succession, falling over each other and piling up like dominos. She had a notebook crammed with notes and observations on the novel.

"Mark's issue is control. What is Sarah's?"

"What do gay men and lesbians have to *say* to each other?"

"Ask Tom: Are gay men who talk about 'humps' exclusively tops?"

The book was very unlike her first two, and sometimes it worried her. The main character was a gay man. She knew she couldn't dictate her material, but she'd assumed after she started writing lesbian material that her themes would remain primarily lesbian. It was the part of her life that was most clear, the words she put down on paper; it was where she exercised control. Deleting bad lines, shifting paragraphs from page to page, reordering chapters, changing someone's name throughout the manuscript with a few strokes of the computer keys. Playing God. On paper, there was nothing she couldn't do.

Novel #1, *Almost There*, published five years earlier, had achieved limited acclaim. The story traced the adventures of Magda Pike on a picaresque journey to lesbianism and self-fulfillment. It was not autobiographical, but more like the life she wished she had had. "A *Rubyfruit Jungle* for the eighties," the best review proclaimed it.

Novel #2, *Mercy Hubbard Slept Here*, followed two years later, a whodunit set in Salem, Massachusetts. Teresa had been reading a lot of mysteries, and her publisher suggested she might try to write one. "Bewitching!" praised a famous lesbian novelist on the back cover.

Then there were a lot of stories she banged out on the computer, one after another, and promptly forgot about. She was just filling time.

About then, Patrick Muller died.

He was not someone she knew well, just a buddy of Jamie's from ACT UP, about her own age. She had socialized with him half a dozen times, always at Jamie's insistence. "I'm having dinner with Patrick, you *have* to come. He absolutely adores you." Or, more casually, "It would mean so much to Patrick if you could join us, sweetie."

She wasn't sure why she meant so much to Patrick, but he did act like her adoring fan. He'd read both her books and proclaimed her his favorite lesbian writer, and he seemed to have read a lot of them.

"You're so good at sex," he said at one dinner, earnestly leaning into her in a way that was not without appeal. He was boyishly clean-cut, small and woman-sized, with lips Tom would call "kissable." "I mean, at writing about sex."

"I could have sworn," Teresa said later, in an embarrassed way to Robin, "that he was coming on to me."

"Then I'm sure he was," Robin agreed. "You know gay men—anything that moves."

Teresa did know gay men, or thought she did. She'd been around them for years through Jamie, Tom, and their circle, but it had always been more like being with girlfriends. There was nothing to question if they rubbed her thigh or kissed her on the mouth. Teresa and her women friends were much more circumspect with one another. Careful hugs and pecks on the cheek were worked up to after months of testing the waters. Will she know it's just friendly? Will she think I want a date? If I ask her to the movies, *is* that a date? Gay men were easier, less complicated in terms of dispensing affection, and her experience was that they dispensed it lavishly and regally, like generous princes scattering coins from the royal coffers.

Patrick, however, was another story. There was something else going on behind his eyes, something that she didn't recognize with men anymore but experienced with women as attraction.

"Oh, God," Jamie said, when she finally mentioned her confusion to him, "it happens all the time. You don't have to want sex with people to have chemistry. From your tone, I thought it was going to be something serious."

She saw Patrick only once after he got sick. His illness was quick and ruthless. He was in the hospital, and she brought him flowers, a big, embarrassing bouquet of pink and white blooms she thought he'd like. The room was brimming with impersonal FTD arrangements.

"You picked these out yourself, I can tell," he said, touched. "You're very sweet."

She blushed and dropped her eyes, then lifted them quickly, ashamed of acting so girlish. She pulled a chair up close to the bed and kept him company while he recounted the horrors of the hospital.

" . . . and the man in the next bed, Mr. Cruz, only speaks Spanish. He's out having tests now. They treat him abominably. The resident doesn't speak Spanish, so he just screams slowly at the poor man. You know, 'Does . . . that . . . hurt?' Then the little faggot has the gall to turn around and be all sweetness to me—you know, because I'm blonde and quintessentially 'American.' I've offered to try to be an interpreter with my high school Spanish, but I can't believe they can't find anyone working in this New York City hospital who's bilingual. They just don't care, that's the bottom line."

His tirade exhausted him, so he asked her to tell him a story. "Tell me about your next book," he coaxed, "in case I don't get a chance to read it."

She sketched for him a mystery she'd had in mind years ago but now had no intention of writing. It made a good story, and it carried him right off to sleep.

Then she didn't see him again.

It wasn't very long before she started her third novel, about the friendship between a gay man and a lesbian, told through the man's voice. The gay man, she assumed all along, was based on Patrick, solicitous, charming, boyishly willful. Somewhere in Chapter Four, the protagonist was diagnosed with AIDS. Again, she thought, the influence of Patrick.

But somewhere around Chapter Six, the character sounded less and less like Patrick. An activist, he delivered eloquent speeches that mesmerized his audiences. A man of deep kindness and compassion, he had a lover of many years and a lesbian friend he worshipped. They formed a pink triangle. By Chapter Seven, it was clear she was actually writing about Jamie.

She was going to make this observation to Robin, but

then Robin left. Teresa couldn't think of whom else to tell, so she kept it as a secret gift for Jamie. She'd dedicate the book to him. No, the dedication would read:

> *In memory of Patrick Muller (1954–1987)*
> *and for Jamie*

She was all the way through Chapter Eight by the time Jamie was diagnosed. And then it was as if her disk drive had crashed. Every day the amber cursor blinked at her accusingly from the black screen. Playing God, it mocked. You writers think you can fuck around with people's lives, pattern characters after friends and relatives. See what you get? Her mother would call it hexing yourself; Robin would say it was "giving yourself a kine-ahora."

Her first instinct was to rewrite the book, deliver the character Mark from AIDS, make it not be true. Hope that life would again imitate art. Maybe then she could hold Jamie in stasis. Some people lived for years with AIDS. One of Tom's friends had shown his first symptoms five years earlier and was still going strong.

But what was holding her up, making it impossible to write, was the realization that the book had to go on. And so did life.

. . .

IN TERESA'S room, the windows were too high for her to see out of. The house was a skinny ranch, and all the windows ran like slits along the upper walls. To look out, Teresa had to stand on a chair. At one time, Alison's bed had been conveniently under one of the windows, but now it was gone.

Teresa's mother didn't like her to balance on a chair, so Teresa waited until she heard the first bars of the music to *The Guiding Light*, her mother's favorite soap opera, and then she dragged her wooden desk chair over to the window.

Teresa was home for the day with a mild head cold. Her

mother kept her home at the slightest hint of illness. Outside it was April, but it didn't look much different from March. The sky was overcast and ready to shower at any moment. There were a few signs of pending spring. On the tree next to the window big pink buds had broken out.

It started to drizzle, then to rain harder, then to splat fat drops against the window. Teresa traced one of them with her finger as it skidded down the glass. She and Alison had a game they played in the car in the rain. They called it Racing Raindrops. They each picked a drop and followed it with a finger across the window. If your drop made it to the other side first you won. Alison had a knack for picking the fastest drops. She always urged them on.

"Come on come on come *on!*"

The game was, in fact, Alison's invention, so it was no wonder she won most of the time.

Alison had other games, too, which were far more intricate. Many involved dressing up and play acting, because she wanted to be an actress. One of her favorites was Peter Pan. Alison was always Peter, Teresa was Wendy, and John and Michael were merely imagined, far less important characters. Tinkerbell was an old flashlight their father let them borrow.

To be Wendy, Teresa wore her blue quilted bathrobe backwards, buttoned behind. Alison had a light green sweatshirt that formed the basis of her costume. She made a hat out of green construction paper rolled into a pointed cap and topped it with a red feather she plucked out of her souvenir Indian headdress from Kennywood Amusement Park.

With the lights out and Tinkerbell streaking and darting around the bedroom, Teresa *was* Wendy Darling, she was about to soar off to Neverland. If she thought about it hard enough and squeezed her eyes shut tightly, the lights of London flickered and danced behind her eyelids.

As she stared out at the narrow, rain-streaked window,

Teresa thought about the TV special *Peter Pan* she and Alison had watched many times, once a year, in fact, for as long as she could remember. The Darling children had a nursery with floor-length windows that opened out onto London. The part of Peter was played by Mary Martin, a grown woman who seemed amazingly boy-like. If you looked hard enough, Teresa's father said, you could see the wires that made her fly, but Teresa didn't want to look that hard.

Alison concocted other play-acting games, too, including the old standby, House. Alison was always the father, Teresa the mother. In fact, in every game they played together, Alison assumed the male role. "I'm older," she explained, "and taller." She had many boyish qualities, a lean physique without a trace of fat, an athletic quality that Teresa envied. Alison preferred imagination games to physical ones, yet she was always finding excuses to jump off the bed as Peter Pan or scale the desk as one of the sons of the Swiss Family Robinson.

They had a lot of books. Teresa, by age seven, was reading years above her grade level because she read everything Alison did. Together they had a subscription to Classic Comic Books, which provided countless sources of play-acting games. Rapunzel. The Princess and the Swineherd. Aladdin and His Lamp. The Magic Pony. Beauty and the Beast. The possibilities had been endless.

Then Alison died, and Teresa had to figure out ways to play alone.

Teresa picked out another fat raindrop and followed it with her index finger as it careened on its zigzag course across the window. "Mine's going faster than yours, Alison," she said to the silence of the room. "I'm going to beat you this time, I know it."

"When elephants fly," Alison snickered.

"No, I mean it."

"When men land on the moon."

The TV clicked off and Teresa heard her mother's slow steps into the kitchen to begin fixing supper. She hurriedly hopped down from the chair and pulled it back across the room, where she sat down at the desk. It was an old school desk her father had procured at a church auction when St. Sebastian's got new furniture for the lower grades. The top had had some knife carvings in it, rude things about teachers and girls Teresa didn't know, mostly about "big" parts of their anatomy. "Mary Lou McKenna has big boobs." "To suck big tits call Felicia San Giacomo." Teresa's father brought the desk home and carefully sanded off all the offensive words. Then he varnished it so there was nothing left but a smooth, shiny finish.

Teresa pulled out a piece of looseleaf paper. This year, in fourth grade, she'd graduated to white from the babyish yellow sheets of third grade. She sharpened a pencil and wrote neatly across the top line, "Carla Carlotta and the Rainy Day."

．　．　．

THERE WAS an evening that Dr. Stanislaus had to come to the house for Teresa's mother. He had cut down on making house calls for his patients, but that night was an exception. He disappeared into Teresa's parents' room with his black leather bag and came out shortly after, looking concerned.

"Tell me what happened," Dr. Stanislaus said to Teresa's father, who stood staring out the living room window while Teresa curled up, terrified, in the big armchair.

"It was . . . I wasn't thinking, I'm so stupid," her father stammered. "I was looking at some old home movies after dinner, just pulling them out to see what was what. I wanted to organize them, and. . . . " He glanced warily at Teresa. "Honey, why don't you brush your teeth and put your jammies on? I need to talk to Dr. Stanislaus."

Teresa peeled herself from the chair reluctantly and padded down the hall. She passed the door of her parents' room, which was closed.

She had seen her mother cry before, but not like that night when her father innocently started sorting through a box of old movies. Teresa had plopped down on the sofa with a fudgesicle, waiting for the show, but her mother remained in the kitchen, excusing herself to do the dishes.

The first movie up was of their last vacation to Lake Erie. "You remember this, don't you, honey?" her father asked. "It was before you could swim. Look how little you were! Eileen, come see how little Teresa was!" Suddenly, Alison ran across the screen in her blue bathing suit, and both Teresa and her father gasped. She pranced in front of the camera, sticking out her tongue, splashing water on the lens. Mesmerized, they both watched her, as if at any moment she might jump right off the screen into the living room.

But then everything faded as the overhead light went on, and Alison became a ghostly outline on the white wall. "How could you do this to me? How could you?" Teresa's mother's face was red and blotchy, and she stared furiously at Teresa's father. "You knew what these movies would be. You knew. What are you trying to do to me?"

"Eileen," her father began unsuccessfully. Teresa stood behind her father as the film flapped off the reel noisily. The fudgesicle began a slow melt onto her hand. Teresa's father flicked off the projector, and her mother stepped forward and reached for the movie. She tore it off the machine roughly and flung it across the room, screaming, "What are you trying to do to me?" until Teresa's father grasped her against his chest. She collapsed onto him, exhausted and sobbing, "What am I going to do?" He put her to bed and called the doctor.

"Eileen," Dr. Stanislaus advised, "would benefit from some counseling." Teresa stood in the door frame of her bedroom, listening to the conversation. Eavesdropping, she had learned, was the best way to get information.

"She won't go," Teresa's father said. "I've suggested it several times, but then she seemed to get better. It comes and goes. She's okay as long as we don't mention Alison."

"It isn't healthy," the doctor warned, "and it's not good for your other daughter, these outbursts. You should all be able to keep your memories of Alison. I can't be rushing over here to give Eileen a sedative every time she's reminded."

"You know she lost both of her parents a few years ago," Teresa's father explained, "in a horrible car crash. Head on, by a drunk driver. She was an only chld, and her parents were loners. She only has us."

"All the more reason to get some professional help," Dr. Stanislaus replied. Teresa peeked around the door and saw the doctor hand her father two slips of paper. "It's what the professionals call cumulative grief, with a lot of guilt thrown in, too. Mothers often experience that after the loss of a child. Here's the name of someone I recommend for counseling, and that's a prescription for a mild sedative, just in case."

After the doctor left, Teresa's father pulled both papers out of his pants pocket, where he had shoved them. One he placed on the coffee table, the other he crumpled and threw away. Then he tucked Teresa into bed with an unusually big hug.

"I know that was a little scary," he said, "but I promise you Mommy will be better soon. She just needs some time. You have to be an especially good girl for a while, okay?"

She nodded weakly and let the blanket envelop her. Her father left the light on in her room that night and for several nights thereafter.

. . .

EVENTUALLY, Jamie stopped working. He'd been cutting back from his real estate job little by little until he phased himself out altogether. His last sale was a one-bedroom co-op in Chelsea to a lesbian and a gay man he knew from his AIDS work who had fallen in love.

"What do you think of that?" he asked Teresa and Tom over dinner in his favorite Japanese restaurant. He accepted the warm hand towel graciously and rubbed it vigorously over his face, turning it a glistening pink.

"You were the one who told me these things happen," Teresa pointed out. "Remember, with Patrick Mullen?"

"Oh, I was talking about flirtation," he corrected her. "Chemistry. That's different. Now we're talking spend-our-lives-together *love*." He drew the word out in a thin line across the table. "I mean, a gay man and a lesbian? What's the point?"

"You know what I think?" Tom said, breaking apart his chopsticks and meticulously smoothing the rough wood. "I think it's not that bizarre. I mean, lesbians and gay men never worked together so much before AIDS. These things happen. People take love where they can get it."

Jamie looked confused. "*I* think," he said, "the whole world's gone crazy." Teresa knew he meant more than the oddity of a gay man and woman in love, but he kept focusing on it anyway. "I mean, when we were younger, everything was clear-cut. Difficult, but clear-cut. There wasn't the blurring of relationships you have now. You were *gay* if you were gay, and that was that."

"When you were younger," Teresa observed, "everyone was closeted."

"When we were younger," Tom added, "there was no open gay community."

"When we were younger," Jamie said, silencing them both, "people died of old age."

He was careful not to eat sushi, though tekka maki had been one of his favorite foods. The newspapers were full of stories of salmonella poisoning, and people with AIDS were particularly cautioned against raw fish. Instead, he ordered chicken teriyaki but eyed Teresa's assorted sushi with envy. Sometimes she considered censoring herself in front of him in little ways, ordering something besides sushi, for example. But she knew he wouldn't want that. Someone had to live normally.

"Not to be morbid," Jamie continued, and Teresa heard Tom take in a quick breath, "but Curtis called me the other day for Eddie Ramos's number. This guy I know from GMHC," he explained in Teresa's direction. "So I said, wait a minute, that's in my other address book, and I went and got it out of my desk. And when I turned to the page to give him the number, you know what? Everyone else under the R's was dead." Jamie paused with a piece of chicken midway to his mouth. "I mean, Eddie was the only one still alive, and he's seropositive."

Tom shot Teresa a look across the table. She took a short drink of her Kirin and let his eyes hold hers in mutual helplessness.

"Well," Jamie inserted into the silence he'd created, "I guess that's not such good dinner conversation, hmm?"

"Don't worry about it," Teresa said, releasing Tom's eyes and staring down into her food. Her stomach burned, and the thought of putting a piece of uncooked fish into her mouth was suddenly repelling. She was already thinking ahead to the days when "Jamie Keenan" would be an obsolete entry in her address book.

. . .

WHEN TERESA went back to school after Alison's death, everyone had forgotten her, even Vivian Masetti, who had sat behind her for two years. They looked at her as cautiously as they looked at Bernadette Doyle, who had just come to St. Sebastian's from a school in New Mexico. Her father was a captain in the air force, and Bernadette had been to three schools in four years. The Doyles did not expect to be in Pittsburgh more than a couple of years.

The difference was everyone should have known Teresa—they'd played with her at recess since kindergarten, sat around her in class, stood next to her during spelling bees. But they acted as if she were a totally new commodity after only a month away, someone, like Bernadette, who had to be watched and tested.

She did look a little different, but so did many of them. Right before returning to school, just a few weeks before her tenth birthday, Teresa and her mother had visited a beauty parlor called "Snip 'n Style" run by a woman named Trix. ("Short for Beatrix," her mother explained when Teresa asked about the funny name she pictured as "Tricks.") Trix had lopped a half-inch off Teresa's mother's pageboy—"just the split ends"—and had recommended a pixie cut for Teresa. For years, Teresa and Alison had both had long, shiny reddish blonde hair that traveled down their backs in waves. Teresa was ready for a change, but as her hair tumbled onto Trix's linoleum, she began to cry.

"It's just hair," Trix chided. She was a gruff woman with a stiff platinum helmet. "It'll grow back in no time."

The finished image in the mirror was disorienting. For as long as she could remember being conscious of her appearance, Teresa had looked pretty much the same. Now a thinner face and bigger eyes stared back at her, a young girl instead of a child.

"See now," Trix said, spinning the chair so her mother could view her handiwork, "a regular young lady."

"My," her mother commented, frowning a little, "it's quite a change. It does make my baby look... well, older." She brushed a hand through it to fluff it up. "Well, if we don't like it, you can just grow it out again."

"That's the beauty of hair," Trix observed, already sweeping the cascades of shorn locks into a neat clump.

Many of her classmates had also made changes. Vivian Masetti looked as if she's visited Trix, too, but her pixie cut curled and frizzed while Teresa's waved. Karen Costello had two big scars on her knees from a fall on cinders. Anthony Pagliatti seemed to have grown an inch at least and was wearing regular neckties instead of bow ties. Raymond Schmidt had his right arm in a cast and was learning to write with his left hand.

Her first few weeks back, Teresa was often sick in class. Once she vomited right under her desk, but the other times she managed to be excused. Finally, it became so frequent that her teacher, Miss Bryant, asked her to stop in to see Sr. Mary Bernard, the principal.

"I have a note for your mother," the nun said, handing her an ominously sealed white envelope. "We're naturally quite concerned about your health, Teresa."

"Please," Teresa said hoarsely, surprised at the raspiness of her own voice, "don't tell my mother." She held the envelope lightly in her hand, extended so the nun could easily take the note back.

"Sit down," Sr. Mary Bernard instructed, taking a seat beside her on the cool green vinyl couch. "Why don't you want me to tell your mother? Teresa, have you been making yourself vomit?"

She knew that was possible; Vivian Masetti had told her she'd done it once when she wanted to miss a multiplication test. But Teresa couldn't imagine anything more disgusting than sticking a finger down her throat.

"No," she said, firmly shaking her head.

"Then why don't you want your mother to know?" A thin hand crept next to her on the couch.

"Because," she replied, watching the veins of the hand pulse beneath the skin, "she'll take me out of school, like my sister. I don't want to die!"

Sr. Mary Bernard's face softened, the hand patted her leg

59

gently. There were several long minutes of quiet, in which only the loud, rhythmic tick of the nun's plain watch could be heard.

"Teresa, you aren't dying," the principal said at last. "But this persistent vomiting is something your mother must be made aware of." She stood up and Teresa lowered the hand that clutched the note. "Make sure she gets that right away." As a parting, Sr. Mary Bernard directed a close-lipped smile at Teresa.

Teresa waited until after dinner, after her homework, after television, when her mother came to her room to say goodnight, to hand her the note. "I . . . forgot to give you this," Teresa stumbled, withdrawing the slightly mangled envelope from under her blanket. "It was in my speller."

Her mother took it from her with a confused look. Silently, she ripped it open with her finger, never taking her eyes from Teresa. Then she read the note carefully, her lips moving slightly, glanced up, and then reread it. She folded it back into the envelope and tucked it away in the pocket of her housedress. Pulling the sheet and blanket up to Teresa's chin, she sighed deeply.

"There's nothing wrong with you, Teresa," she said in a low voice. "You just had a check-up last week. The doctor said you couldn't be healthier, thank God. I don't know why you're doing this. Are you angry with me? Is that it?"

Now Teresa was confused. She almost never felt angry. In fact, she couldn't remember a time when she'd been angry with her mother. Her mother liked everything even and nice, with no disrupting bumps like anger or tears. "There's no need," she often admonished, "to show others your feelings."

"Because it isn't my fault," her mother was continuing. "I know you miss . . . your sister, I know you're sad, but it isn't my fault. I did everything I could. And throwing up isn't going to change anything. It has to stop. It's no good for you. Who knows what your teachers think of us?"

She turned out the light, and Teresa lay awake a while worrying about what her mother meant. She didn't think she could stop throwing up at will, and she wondered what would happen if it continued. Her mother had not elaborated.

Teresa's mother handed her a note the next morning for Sr. Mary Bernard, which Teresa carried to the nun's office. The principal read it before dismissing Teresa.

"I'm glad you and your mother came to an understanding," the nun said, steering her gently out the door with a smile. "Hurry up now, before the bell."

And as if by magic or God's intervention, Teresa stopped feeling sick in class. Actually, she began to feel a lot better the day she and Bernadette Doyle discovered each other on the playground. Neither had been invited into a game of double dutch. Teresa plopped down next to Bernadette on the stone wall, and they watched the game together in silence. Later, when the recess bell rang, Teresa turned to her shyly and said, "I'm Teresa."

"I know," said Bernadette.

.   .   .

HER MOTHER experienced what Teresa later, as a teenager, flippantly called her "atheist phase." After Alison died, her mother, the backbone of Catholicism in their family, abandoned her faith.

The first sign of it was that she stopped attending mass on Sunday, though she insisted that Teresa and her father still go. In the beginning, she made excuses for herself—she didn't feel well, she had too much housework to catch up on. Then there were no more explanations, she just didn't get dressed on Sunday mornings. She remained in her cotton housecoat until well after noon, and when Teresa and her father arrived home from mass, bacon and eggs were waiting on the table with toast buttered and juice poured.

After a few weeks, other signs of wavering faith surfaced. Teresa wasn't sure when it happened, but the statue of Mary that had always been on the buffet in the dining room disappeared. Uncle Jamie had bought it for her mother on his trip to Italy. Teresa always liked the statue; she and Alison had been caught playing with it once, and their horrified mother snatched it away. "It's been blessed by Pope John!" she exclaimed. Unlike the statues at church, where Mary looked tragically morose, Mary in their dining room had a gentle smile creasing her painted lips. Her robe flowed out around her as if in some sacred wind, and the color of it was a sort of violet-blue, not the baby blue of most representations.

Then it was gone.

"I knocked it over accidentally when I was dusting," her mother explained casually when Teresa asked about it. "It was plaster and it shattered to bits."

A crucifix on the wall in her parents' room went the way of the statue. Teresa noticed because its removal left a light cross-shaped shadow on the cream wall. "Look how bad this place needs to be painted!" her mother said, and that became her project for the next weeks. Every day Teresa returned from school and found paint-splattered sheets draping the furniture, her mother on a ladder with roller in hand and dots of yellow or cream or blue on her face, the windows wide open to ventilate the fumes. When she was finished, it was a new version of the same house, familiar and strange all at the same time.

There was still the family Bible on her parents' dresser as a remaining sign of faith, and Teresa had a gold-edged holy card that Grandma had brought her from Alison's funeral. On the front was a picture of Mary in one of her unhappiest moments, and on the back the words that made Teresa's throat tighten when she looked at them: MARY

ALISON KEENAN. She kept it in her desk, where her mother never looked, for a long time, with a copy of Alison's fifth-grade school snapshot. In it she wore the blue cardigan sweater with pearly buttons that Teresa loved and had wanted for her own. But her mother packed all of Alison's things into paper shopping bags and sent her father to the Goodwill bins in the A&P parking lot with them, even the fake fur hat Grandma had given Alison for Christmas and that she'd never gotten a chance to wear.

"You don't need more clothes," her mother said, when Teresa asked for the sweater and the hat. "You've got clothes coming out of your ears, your Grandma buys you so many presents!"

Father Donohue came to visit on a Sunday afternoon after the house had been repainted. It had been a long time since he'd been to the house, and then it was to see Alison. Teresa's mother was in the middle of preparing roast chicken for supper, and she asked the priest if he'd like to stay and join them. He did, and Teresa's father turned off the television and offered Father Donohue a cocktail. He took scotch on the rocks.

Father Donohue made Teresa nervous, because he always found ways to quiz her when she least expected it. "And what did Sr. Ignatius Loyola teach you in religion class this week, Teresa?" he'd say, and she would scour her memory for some nugget of catechism. Or, "Do you remember what Jesus had to say about children and the kingdom of heaven, Teresa?" while patting her hair.

She had never eaten with a priest before, and her parents both seemed to be nervous. Everyone ate quietly, while Teresa's father refilled the priest's scotch and he rambled about his years at St. Sebastian's.

"I have to confess," the priest said with a sad shake of his head, "I still prefer the Latin mass, don't you? As long as I have anything to say about it, we'll keep the ten o'clock service in Latin! What do you think, Teresa?"

She shrugged her shoulders and stuffed a piece of chicken into her mouth shyly.

"Why so quiet?" the priest asked, reaching for her hand and covering it with his own.

"Teresa doesn't say much," her mother answered for her, "but she thinks a lot."

"Well," the priest concluded, "she doesn't have to talk. She's a good girl, I can see it in her eyes." The compliment made Teresa's eyes fall to her lap.

Later, she was watching *Walt Disney's Wonderful World of Color* on television while her parents continued to entertain Father Donohue over tea. "You make a wonderful chicken, Eileen," the priest said, "but you know I didn't come here for the food." Teresa's father joined her in the living room, and only snatches of the conversation in the dining room were audible. Father Donohue did most of the talking.

" . . . to lose one's faith . . . "

"Is he angry with me? What did I . . . "

" . . . Jesus's words, 'My God, My God, why hast thou forsaken me?'"

" . . . trust in God's will . . . "

" . . . mass next Sunday?"

When the priest left, Teresa's mother stayed in the kitchen for a long time washing the supper dishes. She seemed to forget about Teresa's eight o'clock bedtime, because she went from the kitchen into the bedroom and closed the door quietly. It was Teresa's father who noticed the time and exercised his authority. "It's bedtime, isn't it?" he asked hesitantly.

"It's only quarter to eight," Teresa said, eyes glued to the television.

"Don't you have to take a bath?"

"I had one last night."

Stumped, her father urged her off the sofa anyway. "Then go brush your teeth and put your jammies on," he said, suddenly more sure of his control. "Hurry up."

Little by little, her mother's faith returned. She started attending mass every few weeks, then every week, and finally began to take communion again. By the time of Teresa's confirmation in sixth grade, Teresa's mother was going to mass several times a week and a new crucifix replaced the one that had disappeared from the bedroom wall. In Mary's place in the dining room stood a statue of Jesus with sorrowful eyes and a bleeding heart.

By then, though, Teresa had misplaced the photo of Alison in the blue cardigan. It slipped into some recess in her desk. Once or twice she made an attempt to look for it, but after a while she forgot it had existed. The holy card she crumpled and threw away one day when her mother wasn't looking.

. . .

TERESA DIDN'T remember exactly when she first knew Jamie and Tom were in love, but she had a vague sense of it long before Liane, her roommate freshman year in college, told her outright. There had been something unspoken about it in her family, a concern without a name. Until Jamie moved to New York in 1970, family members made excuses for him: "A good-looking man like him can have his pick of girls! Why settle down with one?" or "He's taking his time finding the right girl." Sometimes Grandma still harkened back to Jamie's steady girl from eleventh grade: "Marlene Kryszynski—such a pretty girl. I hear she's single again. Made a bad marriage. I think she lives out in your part of town, Jamie." Even a divorced woman, apparently, was preferable to no woman at all. Jamie always smiled and didn't comment.

There was a feeling about the apartment in Pittsburgh

that Jamie and Tom moved to together in 1968 that made it seem like a home and not a way-station where two bachelors crossed occasional paths. It was what made the family uncomfortable.

"What an interesting table!" Teresa's mother commented on their first visit. It was a rough-hewn oak piece, low and squat, that made an ideal coffee table.

"A friend of ours, an artist, made it for us," Tom explained, then quickly amended the sentence. "For this place, I mean, because neither of us had any furniture to speak of. It's really mostly my table, I guess." Then he colored a deep pink and left the room to check the coffee he was brewing.

Teresa's father cleared his throat and her mother said something forced like "How nice" to Jamie, who was left standing perplexed next to the table in question. Teresa, though only fourteen, noted everyone's edginess with interest. She had not yet become familiar with the term "gay," though "queer" was a staple of her vocabulary. It meant "weird" when she said it, but her mother chastised her for using it.

"That's an ugly word," she scolded.

"Everyone uses it," Teresa protested.

"Well," her mother finished, "you're better than them."

Teresa was stunned to find out after Jamie got sick that he had never actually come out to his family in a formal way. He simply became more open. "Tom and I went to Vermont for vacation." "Tom and I bought a summer house." It was, he admitted, the coward's way out. At first he'd been afraid to tell; coming out wasn't commonly done back then, it was something that usually happened inadvertently, not as a matter of pride. Later it seemed unnecessary, since he wasn't hiding Tom and their relationship from them.

"Imagine," he said to Teresa, shaking his head, "a gay activist who hasn't had the experience of coming out to his family. It's ridiculous."

"It's not too late," she said, wondering as she did what possible good it could do now. She was positive they knew from the way, years before, they tried to implicate Jamie in "making" her a lesbian. She had already told her father about Jamie having AIDS and had the unpleasant experience of hearing him say angrily, "It figures." Still, she thought, coming out was something they all had to go through, a rite of passage. Jamie, she knew, couldn't die in peace without having said the words.

She was not there when he called her father, but she heard the recap the following day.

"I simply said, 'I know you already know this, Rich, but I just want to say for the record that I'm gay and Tom is my life partner,'" Jamie recounted eagerly, as if he could hardly wait for the punchline. "Then there was this long pause, like he fainted. He must have been thinking, why do they put me through this? So I said, 'Rich, Rich, are you there?' And he just sighed this enormous sigh and said, 'I'll tell Eileen.'"

"'I'll tell Eileen'?" Teresa burst out laughing. "That's it?"

"That's it," Jamie said. "Then he hung up. Amazing, isn't it?"

"*Truly* amazing," she agreed. She put an arm around his waist and squeezed. "I'm proud of you. Let's see: You're fifty-five years old, politically active for the last eight, married for twenty-five. . . . It's about time you came out!"

"I'd tell Mother," he said wistfully, "but she probably wouldn't recognize me. She'd probably say, 'Oh, I have a son we think is gay. Do you know him?'"

"Yeah," Teresa agreed, "it's too late for Grandma."

He looked at her oddly, with a sad dreamy look to his

eyes that made them seem to melt away. She expected him to say something else about his mother, but instead he smiled wanly and changed the subject.

. . .

ON THE mantle in the living room, Grandma had a picture of her husband in his shirt sleeves, his foot up on the fender of a gleaming Oldsmobile. He looked very tan and handsome, with his hair streaked gold by the sun. He had a wry smile that reminded Teresa of Uncle Jamie's; it looked like he had just heard a really good joke. Teresa had never met her grandfather because he died of a heart attack when she was a baby, but Grandma told so many anecdotes about him, he seemed very real.

Teresa liked to look at the picture whenever she visited Grandma. She couldn't reach it on the mantle, so Grandma would come up behind her, take it down, and say, "He was handsome, wasn't he? That's where you get your good looks. And the red in your hair."

"What did Grandpa do?" Teresa asked, holding the picture while her grandmother talked.

"He was a salesman, like your dad, like your uncles," Grandma answered. "The best car salesman in Pittsburgh. As honest as the day is long. Everyone knew about Square Jack Keenan."

"Huh?"

"That was the name of the dealership—Square Jack's," Grandma said with pride. "For all the square deals he made."

"And he came from Ireland?"

"From Waterford when he was just sixteen. All by himself to make his living," Grandma explained. "He started out selling hardware and kept getting better and better jobs till he got hired by a Model T dealer named Honest Al Curry. And your grandpa was so good at it, he never did anything else till the day he died."

Then Grandma replaced the photo on the mantle with a sigh. "The day I met him, he was getting out of a brand-new blue Model T on Metropolitan Avenue, all dressed up in a white linen suit and bringing daffodils to another girl. It was a Sunday, and his hair caught the light like in this picture. I was walking home from church with a girlfriend, and she said, 'My word, Aggie, look at *that*.' Those exact words. I'll never forget it. I had to follow him around for weeks before he noticed me." Grandma stroked Teresa's hair. "We were married thirty-three years."

"Do you still miss him?" Teresa asked.

The sun glinted off the fender of the Oldsmobile and shone in Grandma's eyes. "Every day of my life," she said.

. . .

AFTER HER grade school graduation, Teresa went with her parents, Grandma and Uncle Jamie to supper at DeConcini's Family Restaurant, where they had celebrated a handful of other big events over the years: Grandma's sixty-fifth birthday, Teresa's parents fifteenth wedding anniversary, both Alison's and Teresa's First Holy Communions.

Jamie was distracted throughout the meal and barely touched his ravioli. He was chain-smoking Lucky Strikes and ordering gin martinis. By dessert, he was fuzzy-headed and sloe-eyed. While Teresa scooped up the last of her spumoni, he leaned toward her ear.

"I'll take you out someplace *really* nice soon," he whispered drunkenly. "Tom and I. We'll have a great time, the three of us. Tonight. . . tonight I'm not feeling so hot. You understand, sweetie? You'll cut your old uncle some slack?"

She didn't understand, but she let it go anyway. She was good at doing that. It was, she reasoned, woman problems or sex problems or something equally intimate that made Jamie want to lose himself to drink. Grandma frowned at him through most of the dinner.

"Since when have you been drinking so much?" she snapped when he ordered his third martini. And after he downed that one, she observed with disgust, "You're a sloppy drunk, James Patrick Keenan, just like your brother Peter."

Teresa had never seen Jamie drunk before. She'd seen him mix himself a highball at her house on festive occasions, but he was always eating then, too, and the drink never seemed to affect him. Her father had one Iron City beer every evening while he watched the news with Walter Cronkite—like a couple of friends sharing the day's events —but that was the extent of his drinking. But she knew what Grandma meant about Uncle Pete. He was so loaded at his own twentieth wedding anniversary party that his two younger brothers had had to put him to bed. He'd been wearing a Pirates cap turned around and kept calling Teresa "my little girl" in a way that made her want to hide from him.

Jamie couldn't finish the fourth martini. Instead he got up and headed quickly toward the bathroom. Teresa's father called after him sarcastically, "Need help?" and Jamie waved him off impatiently. But it was really the phone he'd gone to use. He stayed on it for over ten minutes while Teresa's father settled the bill. Teresa could see Jamie through the plants at the opposite end of the restaurant, leaning against a wall as he clutched the receiver to his ear with one hand and gesticulated wildly with the other.

"What's he doing?" Teresa's mother asked, sobering up. She herself had been a little giddy from one gin-and-tonic.

"It's probably girl trouble," Teresa's father said, though unconvincingly. He stared worriedly over at the phone. "If he's not off in two minutes, we're leaving."

Over ten minutes later, Jamie wandered back to the table. "You go home," he instructed them with a drunken grin. "I'm expecting someone."

Teresa looked into her empty dessert plate. She knew very well Jamie hadn't wanted to be there, and though she tried not to, she felt furious. She was wearing the silver bracelet he'd given her as a graduation gift, a delicate filigree chain, and she had the sudden urge to rip it off and throw it at him dramatically. He had ruined her special day.

"Don't drive till you've had some coffee," Grandma cautioned him sternly.

"I won't," he promised.

Teresa's parents passed him coldly and pushed Teresa ahead of them. At the door of the restaurant, she turned and looked back over her shoulder at him. The waiter was bringing him a cup of black coffee. If only he'd glance up and wink, she thought. Instead, he stared vacantly at a spot of tomato sauce bleeding on the white paper tablecloth.

As they pulled out of the parking lot, a red Karmann Ghia passed them on its way in. No one noticed its driver but Teresa, because they were preoccupied with criticizing Jamie's drinking. But she recognized the curly dark hair immediately as Tom's.

· · ·

"Mea culpa," he said on the phone the next day. "Mea culpa, mea maxima culpa."

She said nothing.

"You're invited to be the dinner guest of Thomas Snow and James Keenan on Saturday, June 22, at seven o'clock. Is it a date?"

"I might be busy," she stalled.

"You might be, might you?" he mocked. "You're fourteen years old, what *might* you be doing?"

"Avoiding you," she said, smiling in spite of herself.

"That doesn't count as anything to do," he rejoined. "Besides, you're crazy about me, admit it."

"I won't," she said.

71

"Well, I'm crazy about you and always have been," he said, "from the first day your little butt came into the world. So you're going to dinner whether you like it or not. Just be ready."

After he hung up, she blushed into the phone.

. . .

TOM'S NOVEL resided in a Barney's shirt box, and it looked much older than its eight years. The frayed sheets of bond paper were covered in tiny, precise printing more suited to a draftsperson than to a professional writer. No one had read the novel except Jamie, and even he hadn't read it in its entirety. Tom was merely showing it to Teresa, not inviting her to read, and he displayed it upside down so she couldn't make out a single word.

"Of course, you'll read it when it's finished," he said, wincing as one of the rubber bands snapped from age. "Though who knows when that will be. I haven't touched it since Jamie got sick. It's all I can do to keep up at work."

He didn't talk much about work. Though he made a lot of money at it, the job embarrassed him. He had written for many of the big television shows, the serious adult dramas that aired after nine o'clock. When Teresa asked, after graduating from high school, if she should consider TV writing as a career, Tom was adamant.

"Never," he insisted. "It eats your mind."

Early in college, as a double English and journalism major, Teresa imagined herself writing exclusives, her by-line on the front page of the *New York Times*. But her assignments for the college newspaper were dull and flat, written hastily and badly researched. It wasn't in her nature to hound people with the who, what, where, when and why of things, to be ready at a moment's notice to follow a lead, to sniff out stories like curious, lingering smells. Teresa preferred to make up stories than to report real life ones.

She ended up as a copy editor for a popular women's magazine, which she thought probably drained her mind just as much as Tom's job did his. She had to steal time before work to write fiction. It was impossible to spend the day patching up articles about balancing children and career or about getting regular mammograms, then try to create her own work at night.

In Tom's job, he was always putting endearments and sexual innuendos into heterosexual mouths. "Just once," he grinned, "I'm longing to make some cop grab his partner's cock and tongue kiss him on national TV. Wouldn't that be a pisser?"

She wondered why he didn't quit. She half-expected him to when Jamie was diagnosed. After all, Tom had been making a lot of money for a long time—surely he could retire early and concentrate on his novel. In the age of AIDS, who knew how much time anyone had? Why spend it writing heterosexual drivel? But Tom continued going to the television studio until the progression of Jamie's illness prevented it. Then he worked at home before he finally took a leave of absence.

"What's your novel about?" she asked him years before, when she was finishing her first. He had never mentioned his until she proudly announced the pending completion of hers.

"It's sort of autobiographical, I guess," he stumbled, looking a little embarrassed, as if other writers didn't borrow liberally from their own lives. "It's sort of about Jamie and me."

Years later, when he pulled it out of his desk to show her what a nightmare it would be to type, she saw that the title was *Solitary Souls*.

"That's nice," she commented. "I like that." What she

thought, however, was how alone it sounded. If it had been singular, it could have described how she often felt about her own life.

"It's from Yeats," Tom explained, not condescendingly but just for her information. "'Some moralist or mythological poet/Compares the solitary soul to a swan.' You know that one?"

"No," she admitted. She was often admitting an ignorance of poetry to Tom, who had everyone from Auden to Yeats at his fingertips. Jamie had told her once that he, too, had learned all the poetry he knew and could quote from Tom.

Tom continued:

I'm satisfied with that,
Satisfied if a troubled mirror show it,
Before that brief gleam of light be gone,
An image of its state;
The wings half spread for flight,
The breast thrust out in pride
Whether to play, or to ride
Those winds that clamour of approaching night.

"I like that," she repeated, not having caught all the words or the full meaning. But he had told her years before, when she was a kid, that to grasp the sense of a poem was enough. She smiled as he finished reciting in his polished, school-boy way, so soft and almost timid compared to Jamie's florid public speaking manner. Teresa was not sure which style she preferred, but she knew that in their own ways she liked them both.

. . .

ONCE, AT the beach house on Fire Island, she'd walked in on Tom and Jamie having sex. She had been visiting for the weekend and had spent hours off by herself on the beach, reading, walking and collecting unusual shells and bits of sea glass. "We're staying in this afternoon," Jamie had announced with a casual wink that suggested sex. So she'd left them for half a day, the entire afternoon, and made her own fun. She was adept at that—how many days had she spent alone as a kid?

She was once again "between lovers." Most of Teresa's life was spent "between lovers." There had been only two men and two women at that time, and later Robin would become the fifth.

"Gosh," Robin had said. "Number Five? I'm really flattered." That had been reason enough to love her.

The beach was crowded with beautiful men, mostly white. They stripped unabashedly and danced into the water; they lay in the sun with their penises in full view. Teresa politely didn't stare. She had never been very fond of penises as body parts; she found them comical. When Andrew Delaney stripped for her freshman year in college and became the first man she had seen naked, she almost laughed. But she resisted the urge, and he fucked her earnestly, with the zeal of an eighteen-year-old. Later, her senior year, there was Matthew, whom she abandoned after a few boring rolls in the hay. The summer of graduation there was Roz, the M.A. candidate, who lasted just until fall, and after a dry spell of several years, Dana, whom she stayed with eighteen months. After another hiatus came Robin. The time in between was just life. People she knew casually asked her, "Are you seeing someone?" and she answered, "Not right now," never letting on that "not right now" was more likely to last four years than four weeks.

She envied people who had sex at will with people they didn't love. She envied others with relationships that spanned decades. She envied Jamie and Tom the most, and she could never admit that finding them *in flagrante delicto* had turned her on.

On the beach she colored a tender rose that would sting her fair skin later, and she plodded back to the house, eyes down on the boardwalk for errant nails and splinters. She stopped on the way to buy a bottle of Bordeaux for dinner. The screen door made a loud clack as she entered, but maybe they didn't hear her. Or maybe they did and decided not to care. Maybe she heard them, too, but investigated anyway. At the half-open door of their bedroom she watched for several long seconds before averting her eyes from the sight of Jamie bent over, his legs spread, with Tom pumping vigorously into him. If they sensed her presence, they didn't let on but finished their business with soft moans. Once in her room, she closed the door politely and sat on the bed, her back flat against the wall, waiting for it to be over. Later she said nothing, but Jamie guessed what had happened.

"Teresa," he said, when she finally emerged from her room and fixed herself a gin-and-tonic, "about earlier..."

"No," she said firmly, "don't. Look, people have sex. I know that. Just because I mostly don't doesn't mean I'm going to chastise you for having sex in your own house, whenever you want to."

They said nothing more about it, but when she retired to bed she thought about the two of them. Her hand wandered down between her legs, and she masturbated to the image of Tom fucking Jamie. Then, embarrassed and ashamed of her voyeurism, she cried herself to sleep.

Until Jamie died, she still thought of them occasionally when she wanted to get off quickly. Sometimes she even imagined them while she was having sex with Robin. It was the surest way to come when she felt tense. She never admitted it to anyone, hardly even to herself. It was something she kept furtively tucked away, like a well-thumbed issue of *On Our Backs* or a trashy one-handed novel.

· · ·

LE COQ D'OR was the nicest restaurant Teresa had ever been in. In fact, when she thought about it, in her fourteen years she had barely been anywhere but DeConcini's on special occasions and a few other family restaurants while on vacation. But none of them had linen tablecloths with more gleaming silver than she knew what to do with, waiters wearing bow ties and crisp white shirts, and a maitre d' who had Jamie's reservation on a list.

"Right this way, gentlemen . . . and lady," the maitre d' winked. He was a small portly man who seemed to recognize Jamie and Tom, though they told her they had only been there once before.

The menus were large black tasseled books with vellum pages, weighty and hard to manage. The dishes were all listed in French with no translations.

"I'm having the same as last time," Jamie said, slapping his menu closed. "What do you think for Teresa?" he asked over her head to Tom.

Tom pondered the menu and decided that the Coq Paillard would be about the best. "You like white meat or dark?"

"White," she replied, wondering what Coq Paillard meant but feeling too shy to inquire.

"Then that's it," Tom smiled.

Jamie ordered Coq au Vin and Tom chose escargots in garlic and shallot butter to start and a medallions of veal entrée. "What's 'coq'?" Teresa asked, her curiosity finally overwhelming her shyness.

"Chicken," Tom replied with a slight smile and a shifting of legs under the table. The waiter brought a bottle of red wine, uncorked it, and poured a fingerful for Tom to sample.

Tom looked up without a word and raised his eyebrows, and the waiter automatically filled his glass and Jamie's.

"This is some place," Teresa commented. "How did you find it?"

"Friends of Tom's brought us here recently," Jamie explained, adjusting his tie. "It's for special occasions. We... Tom and I just decided to move in...to share an apartment."

"Oh," she said, surprised and wondering why that warranted a fancy dinner.

"Well, on to *this* celebration. I already gave you your graduation present, sweetie, but Tom has something for you, too," Jamie smiled.

She smiled back in astonishment. She barely knew Tom. In fact, hearing him discuss and order dinner was the most she'd ever heard him say. His strong silence always intrigued her.

"Oh, it's nothing much," Tom blushed, pulling an envelope from his pocket. "Just a poem." He unfolded a sheet of stationery and cleared his throat.

You shall above all things be glad and young
for if you're young whatever life you wear

it will become you; and if you're glad
whatever's living will yourself become.
Girlboys may nothing more than boygirls need:
i can entirely her only love

whose any mystery makes every man's
flesh put space on: and his mind take off time

that you should ever think may god forbid
and (in his mercy) your true lover spare:
for that way knowledge lies, that foetal grave
called progress and negation's dead undoom.

i'd rather learn from one bird how to sing
than teach ten thousand stars how not to dance

At the end, he folded the sheet carefully, replaced it in the envelope, and handed it to her gingerly. "e. e. cummings," he said. "Happy graduation. Happy...starting high school!"

"Oh," she said, "thanks." She reopened it and read it again to herself. While he was reading it to her, she thought he had written it. No one had ever given her a poem before, not one they'd written, not one someone else had written. It seemed like such an intimate thing.

"It took him *hours* to pick it," Jamie grinned. "Hours."

"Not quite that long," Tom blushed.

"I like it," Teresa smiled, reddening a little herself. She suddenly noticed how good-looking Tom was. "I'm...not sure what all of it means, though," she added hesitantly.

Tom sipped at his wine, and their salads appeared, alert, leafy concoctions with small round tomatoes nestled in them. "That's all right," he said, showing her which fork to use. "You don't have to. It's the *sense* of it that you want."

At that moment she wanted the evening to last forever.

· · ·

SEX WITH Robin had started like firecrackers, then fizzled and sputtered and died a quiet death. They never even talked about its passing, just let it happen, like a neglected plant left to dry up without water. Only after Robin left did Teresa confirm Jamie's speculations.

"Bed death?" he asked, when she finally intimated there had been more happening to destroy her relationship with Robin than she'd let on at first. He said it so matter-of-factly, the phrase coined by the lesbian sexologist, that Teresa smiled in spite of the painful memory.

"Afraid so," she admitted, and he nodded gravely. "It just became less and less frequent, until it didn't even exist anymore. Classic textbook case."

"Did you have fun in the beginning at least?" he asked hopefully.

Teresa remembered the start of their relationship vividly. For the first few months they had sex every night or day, sometimes both, whenever they could get their hands on each other, depending on their schedules. Standing up, lying down, on a table, in the shower, on a chair, in public restrooms. There had been many wild times. One with men's silk ties was particularly memorable, as was another in front of a full-length mirror. By six months it had tapered down considerably, confined to the bed once or twice a week. Robin disliked lingerie and was adverse to sex toy paraphernalia.

"You don't need this kind of stuff," she protested when Teresa brought home a thirty-dollar dildo to boost their sex life. "If you want to get fucked, why are you with a woman?" The dildo got packed away for a time when she found the courage to try it on herself.

"You should have sex," Jamie said almost angrily, not that long before he died. "You take it too much for granted."

"Don't tell me what I should do," she rejoined. But ultimately she thought he was probably right. Life went by too quickly, and to spend most of it sleeping alone seemed to be a flagrant disrespect.

. . .

LIANE LEVIN suggested they take the bunkbeds apart and face their desks into each other in the center of their large room.

"That way we can make faces at each other while we study," she smiled mischievously. But in the first semester of college that Teresa knew her, Liane rarely opened a book.

Liane's father was Jewish, her mother Catholic, but amazingly she had not acquired the hang-ups of either of those religions. Her father had wanted her to go to NYU or another nonsectarian school, but her mother won out and Liane ended up at Fordham, the Jesuit university in the Bronx, as Teresa's freshman year roommate. Liane herself would have preferred Barnard—"all those *girls*"—but she acquiesced, not caring much about college at all. "They're not happy about my sexual 'tastes,' shall we say," Liane told Teresa the first day they were roommates. "I got caught sucking face with my best friend Monica when I was thirteen."

Liane's entire wardrobe consisted of two oversized gauze skirts that she wore with tee-shirts and no bra. Her nipples were always poking out of her thin shirts, drawing Teresa's eyes directly to them like a magnet. Teresa imagined that Liane was getting lots of stares and catcalls, with men outnumbering women on campus by about seven to one, something Teresa hadn't known when she accepted admission.

Liane never read her assignments. "I want to be a filmmaker, and they expect me to read calculus, for Christ's sake," she groaned. "I should be out... making films!"

She had a Super 8 movie camera, a newer model than Teresa's father's, and Liane seemed to spend all her allowance on film. Liane's father had presented her with a credit card for emergencies, and with it she bought a projector for viewing the films. "This was the biggest fucking emergency *I* ever saw," she grinned as she unpacked it. "All these movies and no projector!"

Liane was always trying to coax Teresa to cut class and star in her three-minute movies. Sometimes she obliged. There was one called *Teresa Tarts It Up*, in which they made her up like a prostitute, complete with satin short shorts borrowed from a fashion-unconscious girl on the third floor. Teresa's favorite was one of her making faces in the mirror over the sink in their room. It captured the way she felt sometimes, split in two—body and emotion. The concept was hers. "Our first real collaboration," Liane said proudly when it came back from the processing lab, and they called it *Teresa Times Two*.

They held movie viewings in the dorm lounge on a wide

wall with long angular cracks that Liane thought enhanced her art. Teresa made popcorn with so much butter people needed a stack of napkins to wipe it all from their hands and mouths. Their other favorite movie snack was Archway oatmeal cookies slathered with Betty Crocker ready-to-spread vanilla frosting. In the first two months of college, Teresa gained almost ten pounds.

Teresa envied Liane's freeness with her body, the way she walked from the hall bathroom in just a skimpy towel and dried herself openly in front of her roommate and whomever else happened to be present. Teresa had never seen another girl naked before except Alison, who had been too young to have breasts or pubic hair. Liane pampered her body, toweling each crevice lovingly and anointing herself with different creams and oils. Teresa still dressed in the narrow space between her bed and the closet with her breasts turned to the wall.

"You're so Catholic," Liane observed dryly, not bothering to elaborate. When Teresa asked, "What do you mean?" Liane just shrugged and said something in French.

There were many nights that Liane didn't come home and didn't explain or talk about it. *"Ma pauvre innocente,"* she smiled, lightly fingering Teresa's cheek, "you don't *really* want to know."

But she did. In fact, Teresa sometimes imagined walking into their room and catching Liane in the middle of sex. The picture of what she would be doing, however, was blurry, and the gender of the person she would be with was equally unclear. The word around the dorm was that Liane "did it" with women *and* men, though she preferred the former.

And there were many nights that Teresa lay in bed wishing Liane would come through the door and crawl under the sheets with her. It was the physical closeness she wanted, she told herself, but there was a suggestion of something more. Something that went on under the sheets that she was still, at eighteen, a little hazy about. She suspected it had something to do with hands, but she couldn't be sure.

. . .

AFTER TERESA started menstruating in ninth grade, later than most of her classmates, her mother decided to explain it to her.

"I guess," she said, when Teresa started dipping into the Kotex box in the bathroom closet, "we should have a little mother-to-daughter talk."

"They explained things in health class," Teresa said with distaste. The thought of her mother talking about it the way Mrs. Bruno had—eggs and sperm and vaginas and intercourse—sent a shiver of revulsion up her back. Her mother still referred to Teresa's private parts as "down there." "Don't forget to wash *down there*," she sometimes warned her, the "down there" always spoken a decibel lower.

"Oh," her mother said, seemingly relieved when she discovered Mrs. Bruno had beaten her to the punch on menstruation, "well then." Teresa stood in the doorway of her bedroom, waiting to shut out the uncomfortable conversation. "But I just want to make sure you know a few other things," her mother persisted.

Her mother stepped over the line where the gold wall-to-wall carpeting of the hallway met the blue of Teresa's bedroom. She sat cautiously on the edge of her single bed and tapped the spot next to her for Teresa.

"You're on your way to being a grown-up woman," her mother said. "You know this means you can have babies now."

Teresa nodded and lowered her embarrassed eyes.

"But the church teaches that there should only be babies in marriage, that men and women shouldn't be together that way unless they're man and wife," her mother continued, biting her bottom lip. "I was almost twenty-one when I married your father, and he was the first for me. It's no sin to wait, it's a sin not to. That kind of love between a man and wife is a sacred and beautiful thing. Anything else is just wrong."

Teresa pulled nervously at a loose thread on her pants, and her mother urged her hand away.

"Stop that," she said. "You're growing so fast we can't keep you in clothes, and you're going to pick them apart!" Her mother sighed and resumed her prepared speech. "You understand what I mean, don't you? About men and women?"

"*Yes*, Mother," Teresa answered impatiently, though she actually had very little idea at all. She had never seen a boy's penis; she'd never even peeked between her own legs. The blood that had begun to flow once a month was still an enigma to her. She only knew it was something that caught her and other girls unawares, that Nora Malone had gotten stains all over her skirt one day in algebra class and had to leave at lunch time in tears and shame.

"Good," her mother finished, standing up. "I just wanted to make sure you understood."

Closing and locking the door after her mother, Teresa turned on her record player and played the Beatles' *Abbey Road* album. She lay on her stomach on the bed, staring at the yellow wall, conscious of the Kotex pad between her legs, like a small, soft pillow. With a gentle rhythmic rocking motion, she pressed herself against the bed until a window of warmth opened in her body. She had no idea what she was doing, though she was pretty sure that if it felt that good, it was probably a sin.

. . .

"YOU NEED some new clothes," Liane announced one Sunday, "to surprise Jamie." They were going to Manhattan to visit Tom and Jamie for lunch.

"What's wrong with my clothes?" Teresa asked suddenly, staring with alarm at her frayed blue jeans, her gold and blue Fordham tee-shirt.

"They're fine, for a suburban Pittsburgh teenager," Liane said, dismissing them with a brush of her hand. "But in New York you need to make more of a statement. No one wears those elephant pants in New York, Tee." Liane was the first person since Alison to give her a nickname.

Teresa hadn't really noticed that elephant-leg pants weren't fashionable in New York, and no one else had commented on her wardrobe. With Liane's credit card they bought tight, straight-legged Levi's and an oversized man's shirt that Teresa forced into the jeans, holding her breath to zip them up. A silk tie with helicopters on it completed the ensemble.

"You look so butch," Liane said, pleased with her choices.

"So...what?" Teresa asked. Her vocabulary was painfully lacking in certain areas.

"Never mind," Liane smiled slyly. "It's probably better if you don't know."

Jamie was indeed surprised, staring at Teresa for several long seconds before greeting her. "Sweetie," he said finally, kissing her cheek, "you...you've changed your look."

"Liane did it," Teresa acknowledged.

Liane and Jamie exchanged a glance that Teresa understood less than the word "butch."

After, when they were walking crosstown through the park, Liane said wistfully, "I think I'm falling in love with your uncle."

Liane plopped down suddenly in the grass and began filming a stretch of empty path.

"He's much too old for you," Teresa pointed out with concern. "He's thirty-eight."

"And I'm the wrong sex, too," Liane said, and Teresa did

a double-take. She had never wondered much about Tom and Jamie's relationship, she took their closeness for granted, though everyone in the family labeled it odd when the pair moved to New York together. Jamie's name had drifted out of family conversations.

Liane filmed patiently, waiting for subjects to come into view. Finally, a small boy on a bike with training wheels wobbled by, his thirtyish father puffing along behind him.

"Anyway, age is irrelevant. They're such a sexy couple," Liane gushed. "Tom fucks Jamie with his eyes." While Liane waxed pornographic, Teresa considered Jamie and Tom. How naive could she be, and when was she going to grow up? There was an embarrassingly long list of words she had never heard until Liane used them: cunt, pussy, blow, head, cum, rim. Sometimes Liane got tired of explaining, and the words went into the definition void. No one in Teresa's high school circle had used anything more salacious than "fuck," and that rarely. Now Liane was telling her she'd missed a vital truth about her own uncle—he was gay—and Teresa had never felt more stupid and foolish. Next she had to admit that she wasn't sure what gay men did together in bed.

"Why, they butt fuck, of course," Liane said, matter-of-factly. "And suck each other off. What did you think, *ma pauvre innocente?*"

Liane jumped up from the grass and started running and filming at the same time. "Come on, Miss Tee—art calls us!" She raced toward the long, white expanse of the Metropolitan Museum, but Teresa took her time catching up.

Jamie and Tom—Teresa had never thought of either of them as sexual. Suddenly, just like Liane, they were.

. . .

LIANE WAS familiar with the subways, having grown up in Manhattan and taken trains and buses by herself since she was ten or eleven. "Kids in New York grow up fast," she mused, when Teresa related her own suburban childhood of being driven to school every day by one of several carpooling mothers. In high school, a yellow bus stopped right at the Keenans' front door. "Spoiled," Liane snickered. "Positively coddled."

Teresa followed Liane onto the D train at Fordham Road and out of the car at the Tremont Avenue stop. She had herself not bothered to glance at the subway map, but trusted Liane's expertise in matters of public transportation. "I could be taking you anywhere," Liane observed, amused at the thought. "I could take you to Canarsie, for God's sake, and you'd just follow me. Really, Tee, it's time to learn the ropes of living in New York."

But that day was for learning other things. Liane led her along Bronx streets that were deteriorated by time and poverty, where several entire blocks looked like pictures of wartime Europe. In a storefront on one of the less ravaged blocks was the sign "WOMEN'S HEALTH CLINIC" with a plant in the window beneath it. Inside was a waiting room full of black and Latina women.

"The best place to get birth control," Liane had informed her. "And the cheapest. An exam costs five bucks." Teresa hadn't really wanted any birth control of her own, but she had shown curiosity about Liane's diaphragm when she saw it lying out on her dresser.

"What's this?" Teresa asked, suspecting but unsure. Next to its flat container was a half-squeezed tube of Ortho jelly.

"My goddess, my salvation," Liane said, dramatically waving her arms and wrapping them around Teresa, forcing her into a dance around the dorm room. "I'd be in *big* trouble without it. And I do mean *big*." Liane stopped suddenly and eyed her inquisitively. "Don't tell me you don't know anything about birth control either!"

Teresa sighed and turned her head away, embarrassed,

but Liane took her chin firmly in hand. *"Ma pauvre innocente,* it's nothing to be ashamed of! The Pope should be castrated, for what the Catholic Church does to girls."

Liane decided it was definitely time for Teresa to see a gynecologist and acquire her own diaphragm. "You never know when you'll need one," she advised. "Why, any day now you might get the urge to bust your cherry, and guys can't be trusted to think about anything responsible when their cocks are hard."

They sat in the stuffy, humorless waiting room for over an hour, while children played at their feet and conversations in Spanish whizzed past them. Liane blew her bubble gum into huge, balloon-shaped membranes while Teresa skimmed two-year-old copies of *Ladies Home Journal.* Once, Liane ventured down the block to buy them each a Fresca and returned just as the receptionist was calling Teresa's name.

"You can't come in," the woman said to Liane. "You have to wait your turn."

"I'm just here for moral support," Liane said. "We're a team."

"Sorry," the woman said, motioning to Teresa, who waved sadly over her shoulder to Liane and disappeared down the corridor with a nurse to an examining room.

"Take everything off, put the gown on, open in front, and lie down on the table with your feet in the stirrups. The doctor will be right in."

It was an absurd position to be in for even a minute, but for close to ten minutes, it was torture. As soon as Teresa decided to sit up, however, the nurse returned with a male doctor. "I told you to put your feet in the stirrups!" she reprimanded.

"I did, but . . . "

Teresa resumed the humiliating position, her exposed

crotch greeting the middle-aged doctor. "This is your first pelvic exam, Miss . . . ?"

"Keenan," the nurse said.

"Keenan," the doctor repeated.

"Yes," Teresa replied, "it is. My first."

"Are you sexually active?"

"No," she said. Then, because that sounded ridiculous at a birth control clinic, she added quickly, "Not yet."

Before she knew what was happening, rubber-gloved fingers were up inside her, the doctor's left hand pushing at her abdomen. Withdrawing his hand but without saying anything in preparation, he inserted something cold and metallic inside of her and started cranking.

"Ow," Teresa said, every muscle in her lower body tensing.

"Just relax," the doctor said, "this will only take a minute. It'll be over before you can say 'speculum.'"

Later, she sat on the table clasping the tissue-paper gown to her like she was a hastily wrapped present. "The nurse will advise you about the various birth control methods available. I always recommend the Pill, for sheer spontaneity." And with those few words of wisdom, the doctor exited. The nurse brought out an illustrated chart of options, and when Teresa chose the diaphragm without hesitating, fitted her and showed her the basics of using it.

"It'll take some practice to get it right," the nurse said. "Like tampons." What Teresa didn't divulge was that she still used napkins, not tampons, and had never even dared to look at her own private parts.

She emerged into the waiting room with her new possession and paid five dollars at the desk. "Well? Well?" Liane asked expectantly. "You got it?"

Teresa waved the plastic case in front of her with a smile. She had no plans to use the contents—in fact, she hardly knew how—but the thought of carrying it in her bag sent a charge of excitement between her legs.

"Today," said Liane as they left the clinic, "you are a woman."

Back in their dorm room, Liane asked if she knew how to use it correctly.

"The nurse showed me, sort of," Teresa said, not bothering to look up from her French literature reader. Her vocabulary was not very good, and Liane had to explain to her the nuances of Colette's *Claudine à l'Ecole*.

"Sort of?" Liane winced. "Sort of doesn't count. Do you want a demonstration?"

Teresa nodded hesitantly, her book open in case she needed a quick retreat. Liane closed the door of their room with a sly glance at Teresa and locked it.

"We don't want any of those nosy prudes down the hall coming in," she said. "They already say so many vile things about me, like that I do it with animals. Can you believe it?"

Liane kicked off her bikini panties from under her skirt. They were so small, Teresa wondered why she bothered to wear anything. Still watching Teresa, Liane opened her diaphragm case and removed the rubbery disk.

"First, you squeeze a little jelly right here," Liane illustrated. She hitched up her gauze skirt and bent her knees. "Then you insert it, like so." Her long fingers pushed the diaphragm inside her until it disappeared from sight. "You have to get it around the cervix, or it doesn't work."

Teresa didn't know where to put her eyes next, so she stared back into her book. "I think I've got it now," she said, her cheeks flushed.

"Do you?" Liane asked, dropping her skirt and approaching Teresa's desk. "Do you? Maybe you should try it, too. I'll make sure you do it right."

"No, that's okay," Teresa said quickly. "I don't even know any guys here I'd want to screw around with."

"But what if you met someone tomorrow?"

"I'll remember what you told me. Make sure it's around the cervix," Teresa said, knowing Liane suspected she had no idea where the cervix was.

"*Ma pauvre innocente,*" Liane said, running a finger coyly down Teresa's nose. She crossed the room and picked up her bag, a large drawstring patchwork of differently colored leather squares.

"Where are you going?" Teresa asked with surprise. She liked best the evenings Liane didn't go out wandering but stayed in the room and tossed new ideas for films Teresa's way.

"Since I took the trouble to put this sucker in, I might as well use it," Liane replied casually. "I guess that means a boy tonight. Ta-ta, chérie."

Liane didn't bother to close the door after her. She also, Teresa noted, didn't bother to put her underwear back on.

. . .

AFTER LIANE flunked out in December, Teresa had the room to herself. For the first few weeks, it was very lonely; then she became reaccustomed to having her own room. Some nights she slept in her bed, other nights in Liane's. The nights in Liane's bed she thought about her, wondered where she was and who she was with, and if her father had punished her for flunking by taking away her credit card. Teresa rubbed herself vigorously against Liane's pillow and, just moments after she came, burst into big, hot tears. Liane had gone without saying goodbye, but she typed a note on Teresa's typewriter and left it in the roller.

> *Ma pauvre innocente,*
> *You must go on without me. I hate a scene. My old man is cumming to take me away, ha-ha. Do not cry, chérie. I bequeath to you my cherished projector and*

some bee-yootiful films. Take care of them and yerself.
Always remember: Boys can stick it, but girls can lick it.
   Yer pal,
   Liane

A month after Liane left, Teresa had a visitor. She usually left her door open when she was in the room, so she could hear other girls coming and going, or so they'd drop in to say hi. Not many did. Teresa and Liane's movies were popular, but *they* weren't particularly. They spent too much time together, and Liane had an unsavory reputation. After Liane flunked out, Teresa found she had to start from scratch, talking to more people in class, visiting girls on her hall. It was hard work for someone whose first inclination was to be alone. Sometimes she gave it up and spent time with Jamie in Manhattan. But he encouraged her to keep at it and finally told her bluntly that she was visiting him too often.

The day of the visitor, she was writing a story called "Jackie," about an oddball girl in a college dorm who was misunderstood by everyone but her closest, somewhat square, friend.

How long he had stood there clearing his throat she wasn't sure. A gangly young man wearing wire-rimmed aviator glasses, a blue plaid shirt and jeans with work boots, he bore a vague resemblance to the news editor of her high school paper. His straight brown hair brushed the collar of his shirt. He was so thin his chest seemed to have sunken in from the weight of something resting on it, and his jeans rode low and almost off his hips.

"I'm looking for Liane," he said finally.

Teresa must have looked confused, because he continued quickly, "Liane Levin. Isn't this her room?"

"Oh," Teresa said, slowly catching on, "it was. She left. Flunked out." Why she added that she wasn't sure, except that he had an unnerving intellectual air.

"Huh," he grinned. "Big surprise." He ambled in uninvited and held out his hand, which was large and firm and out of place with the rest of his delicate body. "I'm Andrew Delaney, a friend of hers."

She stared at him quizzically, wondering how a friend couldn't know that Liane had left.

"Well, not exactly a friend," he added, reading her hesitation. "We used to get stoned together sometimes. And... well, you know. She got good weed from some guy on Webster Avenue."

This was information Teresa didn't have about a whole other life Liane had had. Again, she felt foolish and innocent. She'd never smoked pot even once. And what was the "you know" about? Was Andrew one of the reasons Liane didn't come home some nights?

"You don't happen to know who he was, do you?" Andrew asked, nervously brushing his hair from his face. "The guy she got it from?"

"No," Teresa said, wishing she did, wishing she had shared that part of Liane's life. She noticed he didn't ask where Liane was, just the dealer.

"Shit," he said, with a fierce shake of his head that sent his hair falling back across his glasses. Suddenly, he seemed to forget the subject of marijuana and smiled disarmingly. "Who are you, anyway?"

"Teresa Keenan," she introduced herself hesitantly, offhandedly, as if she didn't want to. But she talked to him for close to twenty minutes anyway.

Later she lay in bed remembering the way he tossed his hair.

. . .

HE SHARED a suite with three other freshmen, so it was in her room that she first let him fuck her.

"Oh-h-h, oh-h-h . . . baby," he shuddered on top of her, while she waited for something to happen for her, too, like it did when she rubbed against Liane's pillow. She was uncomfortable and it hurt a little, and when he slipped out of her, she felt lonely.

"You didn't make much noise," he whispered, his face wet against her cheek, his semen leaking out unpleasantly onto her leg. "Did you come?"

"No," she said truthfully. "I don't think so." He looked at her with curiosity, either too young or too self-centered to be insulted or take it personally.

"Well," he smiled lasciviously, "we'll just have to try something different. I'll show you something my last girlfriend liked a lot."

She wrote poems that she let only him see, efforts at pornography that utilized the words Liane had taught her, and he accepted them without really understanding what to do with them. "Thanks, babe," he always said, smacking his lips on hers noisily.

On his nineteenth birthday, which was three days before her own, she gave him a volume of W. H. Auden, who Liane had said was the greatest twentieth-century poet. On her birthday, he bought her a nickel bag on Fordham Road, which they brought back to her room and smoked half of before sex. She never saw him read the Auden, though sometimes he let her read aloud to him.

He had already declared his communications major, wanting since the age of nine to be a broadcast journalist.

"When I saw Walter Cronkite announcing President Kennedy's assassination," he remembered, "I knew what I was going to do."

She was not in love with him, but the sex was fun. It made her feel like a bad girl, not the good girl she had always been, dating boys who never even dared to kiss her mouth. Still it bothered her when he was around the room too much and she needed to study or write. One night he refused to go home or leave her alone.

"I have to finish this paper," she complained, pulling away from him even as he yanked her down to the bed. "It's due at nine tomorrow."

"Later," he insisted. "You have all night." He unzipped her jeans first, roughly, then his.

Pulling free, she slapped him hard with the back of her hand, leaving a mark on his face, startling both of them. "What, are you turning into a lesbian or something?" he jeered as he slammed the door behind him. The last thing she saw of Andrew was his skinny ass. Her Norton anthology hit the door with a thud.

A month later, final exams over, the campus dissolved for the summer into the middle of the Bronx, and she flew back to Pittsburgh, a different girl all together.

"You look older," her mother noticed. "Nineteen already. My baby."

That summer, she attempted to keep a journal of her deepest thoughts, but it turned out she didn't write them down much at all. She tried to write something about Andrew, but it ended up being about Liane. She crossed it all out, then tore the page defeatedly from the notebook.

Once Andrew telephoned on a whim to say goodbye. He sounded fuzzy, like he was drunk or stoned. He was taking a year off to travel across the country interviewing people about the war, an oral history. ("I'll be good at the oral part, huh, babe?") Did she remember the night the Vietnam ceasefire began, when the bells rang out across campus? A clear winter night when students danced on the lawn without coats or jackets, their breath frosty as they cried out their relief?

"How could I forget?" she said simply, just wanting to be off the phone.

It was a summer of very few words.

．　．　．

JAMIE CALLED her after a week in the Pines. The sea air made him feel strong, he said; no, "sturdy" was the word he used. "Like some big tree trunk," he laughed.

"Brent Lynch was lifted out by seaplane," he continued after a pause. "You remember him, sweetie? The tall, good-looking hunk with the tattoo?" The tattoo grounded her; otherwise, "tall," "good-looking," and "hunk" described any number of Jamie's friends. When she met Brent, she remembered staring almost rudely at his tattoo. She'd never seen a real one close up, though Robin had once gotten a fake one at the Christopher Street festival after the Gay Pride March. Brent's was a yellow thunderbolt with the name "Carlos" slashed through it in black. "My former lover," Brent explained, flexing it for her. "Take my advice, honey, don't ever get a lover's name tattooed on you. Love's too fleeting." He said "fleeting" in a whispery voice that didn't match his large, muscular physique.

But Jamie told her later that Carlos was not someone who left on a whim; he'd died nine months earlier.

"Don't you find it a little callous," she asked, "for Brent to say that about Carlos? I assumed it was some guy who dumped him."

Jamie shrugged. "Maybe that's how he sees it," he suggested.

Now Brent was airlifted from the island, and Jamie didn't say any more about it.

"We walked down the beach to the Grove," he did say, switching gears abruptly. "Sweetie, there was a beached whale! You should have seen it. People said they saw it floating in, dead, just bobbing its big hulk on the waves. I wish I'd seen that. By the time we got there, it'd washed up and the marine biologists were on it like flies on dog shit. When we walked up, they had split it open and one of them was reaching around inside saying, 'Jack, I can't find it!' I wonder what they were looking for," he finished wistfully. "Tom speculated that maybe it was Jonah."

She laughed and tried to picture the whale, but she'd only seen them from a distance one vacation with Robin on Cape Cod, their enormous tails made miniature by sea and space.

"It was the biggest thing I'd ever seen," Jamie went on incredulously. "Tom's going to use it somehow in his novel."

She wouldn't remember the story until much later, when Jamie died and decisions had to be made.

"No autopsy," Tom told Teresa. "We know what killed him, and I don't want someone poking around inside him like that, even for the sake of science. It's not fair. It's not . . . worthy of him."

Tom never did use the whale story, not as a metaphor, not even on TV.

. . .

Bernadette Doyle had not always been an only child, but she didn't remember her baby brother. When she was three, he had died from crib death, and her parents didn't have any more children.

Crib death was something new to Teresa. She imagined a crib falling over and crushing the helpless infant. But Bernadette explained that he "just stopped breathing" and that the doctors didn't know why. It happened while everyone was asleep.

"My sister died of leukemia," Teresa offered. She had never come right out and said it before. At home, they always said "passed away." It felt lighter to say it to Bernadette on the playground as they sat getting to know each other, like a pocket of air had opened up inside her. "The doctors don't know why she died either."

"Those doctors," Bernadette said, shaking her curly hair in reproach, "don't seem to know *much*. At least that's what my dad says."

Bernadette invited Teresa to her house after school one Friday to stay for supper and sleep over. But Teresa's mother did not like sleepovers, she thought Teresa was still too young for them. "When you're twelve or thirteen, you'll be at a slumber party every week," her mother noted, but it was hard for Teresa to think past Friday night to two or three years into the future.

Teresa's mother relented to supper at Bernadette's. "But if you don't like something on your plate," she warned, "you'll just have to eat it anyway. It's not like being at home."

Bernadette lived in a white frame house with green shutters four blocks from school. Ringing the house were Japanese maples, their leaves flaming red. "It's the nicest house I've ever lived in," Bernadette said wistfully as they climbed the porch steps. "Sometimes I pray we can stay here forever."

Most of her other homes had been on air force bases, but now her father had dispensation to live off base.

"It's like in the movies," Teresa marveled as Bernadette led her through the living room, filled with comfortable overstuffed chairs and a spinet piano.

"*Rebecca of Sunnybrook Farm*," Bernadette sighed, nodding. "My dad says this was an old farmhouse. All the land around here belonged to it." Bernadette looked dreamy-eyed as she skidded her fingers across the piano keys. "Don't you wish we could have lived back then?"

Teresa smiled, equally dreamy. She often wished she were in another place or time, but she had never met anyone who felt the same, except Alison.

Upstairs in Bernadette's room a colorful braided rug covered the floor, and that was where Bernadette set up the

Mousetrap game. But Teresa would have been content to sit in the padded window seat and stare out at the yard below, which was a sea of pink and white petunias. "This is a pretty room," she said admiringly. "I wish my room was like this."

As they played, Teresa's eyes roved, exploring all of Bernadette's things. Her furniture was painted a pastel yellow, and the bedspread and curtains were a crisp white eyelet. A menagerie of stuffed pets covered the bed, not just the usual dogs and bears, but also elephants and giraffes and kangaroos, so many that Teresa wondered where they went when Bernadette slept. On a shelf near the window rested a collection of foot-high dolls in different costumes of the world. "My dad brings me one from each place he goes," Bernadette explained as Teresa fingered the kimono of the Japanese one. "Korea, the Philippines, Germany, Alaska. He's been everywhere."

Bernadette's mother brought them Hostess chocolate cupcakes and milk. Teresa bit into hers hesitantly at first, saving the frosting for last. Her mother never let her have anything sweet before supper. She licked the foamy white cream from her fingers with guilty relish.

"You get a cupcake after school every day?" she asked in awe.

"No," Bernadette replied, "usually just some cookies. But *you're* here. You're company, so this is kind of special." She nudged Teresa. "Your turn."

Teresa thought the best part of Mousetrap was the plastic mice. Given first pick as the guest, she chose the blue one. She'd never played the game before, and Bernadette beat her easily.

"Who do you play all these games with?" Teresa asked, as they surveyed a chest stuffed with Sorry!, Life, Bingo, Concentration and Clue.

"Sometimes my mom and dad," Bernadette said casually, closing the lid on the treasure trove of games while

Teresa was still taking inventory. "We move around so much, I don't get to have many friends. At least not for long." She opened her mouth to say something else, then snapped it shut. Testing the waters, she said slowly, "I'll tell you a secret if you promise not to tell anyone else."

"Promise," Teresa said with a firm shake of her head.

"Cross your heart and hope to die? Stick a needle in your eye?" Bernadette pressed her.

Teresa remembered how Alison scolded her for making that pledge. "I don't like to say that," she frowned, "but I promise not to tell."

"Sometimes," Bernadette whispered, "I pretend."

"Pretend what?" Teresa pursued.

"That there's someone else to play with," Bernadette admitted, shyly casting down her eyes. "You know, a friend." When Teresa said nothing, Bernadette bravely continued. "Her name is Jill. She has a big family, and she . . . looks a little bit like you!" she ended with a nervous giggle.

This time Teresa's mouth popped open, but she closed it tightly over the words, "I pretend, too." She had never shared that with anyone, that she sometimes talked to Alison and pretended she was still alive, telling her stories at night and playing games with her when she was lonely. Teresa suddenly ached for her sister and couldn't say any more to Bernadette's revelation than "oh." Her friend's confession, so pure and honest and uninhibited, accentuated her own aloneness and made her feel like crying. "I have to go to the bathroom," she blurted out, and Bernadette pointed the way down the hall.

Once safely behind the bathroom door, Teresa burst into tears. To cover the sound, she ran the faucet, a trick she'd learned from her mother, who sometimes stowed away in the bathroom with the door locked. If Teresa held her ear quietly to the door, she could hear her mother's sobs through the flow of the tap water.

Teresa rubbed her eyes furiously and flushed the toilet, even though she hadn't used it, figuring Bernadette might notice if she didn't flush. When she emerged into the hallway, Bernadette wasn't around, and Teresa descended the stairs to the first floor. Bernadette was helping her mother set the supper table. She seemed vaguely embarrassed and would only look at Teresa furtively in short, sideways glances.

Her mother asked, "Are you all right, dear? Would you like to go home? Captain Doyle can take you as soon as he gets here. Bernadette didn't mean to upset you, did you, Bernie?"

Humiliated, Teresa shook her head to the offer of a ride home.

While Bernadette laid out the plates and napkins, Teresa watched and politely answered a string of questions from Mrs. Doyle, who looked at her cautiously and kindly.

"What does your father do?"

"Where do you live?"

"Do you have any brothers or sisters?"

"No," Teresa said shortly, without explaining, but Bernadette took it a step further.

"Her sister had leukemia and died a few months ago," she noted, carefully setting the forks in their places.

"Oh, my dear," Mrs. Doyle said quickly, "I'm so sorry."

"It's okay," Teresa said automatically.

The Friday supper fare was unlike any at Teresa's house, where they usually ate fish sticks with Kraft macaroni and cheese. Mrs. Doyle served scrambled eggs, fried potatoes and toast, just like Sunday breakfast. All the Doyles smothered their eggs in Heinz ketchup, and Teresa tried not to look at their plates, for fear of throwing up.

Captain Doyle talked all through supper with his mouth full. He had a hefty laugh that grew bigger with each Iron City beer he drank. He told stories about the base that Teresa didn't understand, and he ate second helpings of everything in his uniform with a napkin tucked into his neckline to protect the front.

After dinner, Bernadette demonstrated her skills on the piano. She fumbled in the middle of "Beautiful Dreamer," but her father encouraged her to go on.

"You're getting better, baby, keep it up," he winked over the *Pittsburgh Press* sports section.

"You can try, if you want," Bernadette coaxed Teresa, who had never touched a piano key and badly wanted to. She brought one tentative finger down on a black key and smiled at the sharp note. But by the time Teresa had experimented with several more, picking out a tune of her own invention, her father was at the door to take her home.

"Ready?" he asked, and she was suddenly glad to see his familiar face, his soft eyes that resembled clear green ponds when he was feeling tender. She needed to be away from Bernadette and her dolls, her games, the shadow of her make-believe friend, the sharp and stinging memory of Alison.

"See you Monday," Bernadette called with a wave from the darkened porch, a few early fireflies twinkling pinpoints of light. But they both seemed to guess their tenuous connection was already frayed. Bernadette couldn't have known why, except perhaps to think Teresa found her fantasy friend odd. Teresa couldn't tell why either, but she went immediately to the desk in her bedroom and angrily ripped her latest story about Carla Carlotta finding her long-lost sister into tiny, unreadable pieces.

. . .

TERESA AND Gloria Rosa had become friends immediately. They worked together at the magazine for two years, until Gloria took another job. Their desks adjoined, and they had to either like each other or endure the daily torment of face-to-face contact.

"I thought I'd made a big mistake taking this job," was the first thing Gloria said to her when they met, "until I saw your coffee mug." Teresa smiled and tipped the mug that read "Lesbian and Gay Community Services Center" toward Gloria in welcome. Gloria plunked down her style guide, Webster's dictionary and supply of blue pencils onto the desk across from Teresa. "Lots of high heels around here, huh? But it's okay to be out?"

"Nobody seems to mind much," Teresa said. "Margaret, the boss, is cool. I didn't bring the mug out right away. I eased them into it."

"Margaret says you've been here five years, and that I can ask you anything. You must've seen a lot of people come and go," Gloria mused. "Any other dykes?"

"Yeah, one at least, but she really wanted to write health articles and was pretty unhappy copy editing. I think she lasted a month."

"What's the secret of your staying power?" Gloria asked with a grin.

"I don't know," Teresa said. "None of this means much to me. It's just a job." Then with a smile, "What would you say, lack of ambition?"

They started taking lunch together, turkey and provolone sandwiches that they carried to Bryant Park in the mild spring weather. Gloria liked to eat in the shadow of the New York Public Library.

"Someday, girlfriend, your books will be there," she told Teresa. "Think of it—your name in the card catalog! Keenan comma Teresa."

"Yeah, I don't know," Teresa said doubtfully. "I'm not sure when the Public Library will be ready for *my* books."

About a month after she started working for the magazine, Gloria called in sick. It was a particularly long day for Teresa, staring at the vast expanse of Gloria's desk while she doctored the prose that came across hers. Teresa didn't know why she had stayed in a dead-end job so many years, except out of habit and disinterest. She was good at her job and did it quickly. As a copy editor, she put in eight hours a day and rarely more, and her morning arrival time had become flexible. That gave her an hour and a half before work to write fiction while her mind was clear of health and beauty tips.

Having Gloria there made the job less mundane. "Hey, how are you?" she asked when Gloria returned to the office. "It was quiet around here without you." She almost said, "I missed you," but wasn't sure how it would sound to Gloria.

"I'm shitty," Gloria said. Her eyes were puffy and red, like she was suffering from a severe allergy. "Alicia and I broke up."

Gloria had talked a lot about her girlfriend, Alicia Vargas, at her lunches with Teresa. Alicia and Gloria had been together since college, ten years, and had recently found they'd grown up and apart. It was a source of amazement to Teresa, who thought there should be some universally agreed upon cut-off date after which couples didn't have to fear breaking up. Five years? Seven years? Ten years with someone and you still couldn't be sure? It was too sad to think about.

"I need to get out of the apartment," Gloria said. "You know anyone who's looking for a roommate?"

"Stay with me," Teresa offered immediately, without considering how it might affect their new friendship to work *and* live together. "There's just a pull-out sofa, but it'll be okay until you find something," she added quickly.

It took only a few days for the apartment to feel like it was caving in on Teresa. She could have sworn the rooms were smaller when Gloria was staying with her. As her contribution to the living arrangement, Gloria prepared dinners from a small repertoire of Puerto Rican dishes she'd learned from her mother—rice and beans cooked with pork, its tantalizing aroma wafting through the apartment, fried plantains that turned liquid on the tongue. While it was good to eat so well and with someone, Teresa also liked saying goodnight and closing her bedroom door. In just a week's time, she was running out of things to say to Gloria over dinner. They couldn't share their days at work, because they were already intimate with each other's jobs. They had chronicled their sexual and relationship histories, complained about their families. Teresa started asking around more energetically about apartment shares for her friend.

Gloria didn't seem to experience any strain, but then she was used to living with someone. It began to feel almost like she had settled in and had no intention of leaving.

"Any luck today with apartments?" Teresa asked hopefully but lightly over their desks.

"I had a lead that fell through," Gloria said nonchalantly. "I guess it takes time. Hey, I thought I'd make arroz con pollo tonight. How does that sound?"

"Oh," Teresa said, glancing up briefly from her copy. Why did she suddenly not know how to spell "aerobics"? It looked all wrong to her on the manuscript. "I . . . I have a dinner date tonight. I won't be home till late."

"You're holding out on me, girlfriend," Gloria grinned, but there was a quiver of disappointment in her mouth. "Who's the babe?"

"I really don't want to talk about it," Teresa said abruptly, mostly because there was no date and no babe. In fact, she had invited herself over to Jamie and Tom's because the closeness with Gloria felt like she was being bear-hugged by someone who didn't know her own strength.

"She wants to do everything with me. She just seems to

like me too much," Teresa told Jamie, worriedly.

"Heavens," he mocked, "how horrible!"

Gloria was watching *The Tonight Show* in the dark when Teresa got home from Jamie's. The break-up with Alicia had made her an insomniac, and she routinely stayed up until one or two o'clock.

"This is late for you on a school night," Gloria commented. "Must have been some date!" She said it with a forced levity that suggested she knew the truth.

"Hmm," Teresa said, yawning. "Can I tell you some other time? I've gotta sleep."

"Teresa?" Gloria called after her, and Teresa turned. Her friend looked shy and vulnerable in the light from the TV screen, and her voice was softer than usual. "I really appreciate you letting me crash here, but I was thinking I'd go to my friend Alma's on Thursday. Spread myself thinner, you know? That okay with you?"

"Sure," Teresa said, the guilt rising in her like a bubble. "Whatever you want. But you're welcome to stay." She walked to the couch and sat down next to Gloria, helping herself to popcorn from the bowl in her friend's lap.

Gloria smiled and munched quietly. "Thanks," she said through a mouthful.

Teresa leaned back and put her feet up on the trunk she used as a coffee table. "Who're the guests tonight?" she asked.

· · ·

SHE LOVED Robin, but there were times when she wanted her to go home.

Once after weeks of almost constant companionship, Teresa and Robin planned separate evening activities. "I think I'll have dinner with Donald," Robin said on the phone. "What'll you do?"

"Read, I think," Teresa said. "Maybe cook dinner for a

change. Clean out the leftover Chinese food containers from the fridge."

"Don't go gluing yourself to the TV," Robin chuckled. "Who knows what you'll do when I leave you alone!"

Teresa could have said the same thing. They were nearly two years into their relationship, sex had slowed to something that might happen every few weeks, and Teresa couldn't help but notice how Robin talked to other women, studying their mouths. It was risky, Robin having a night on her own. She was an infidelity waiting to happen. But since Teresa rarely had time to herself, it was a chance she had to take.

Teresa stopped at the supermarket after work for the ingredients for lemon chicken. It was odd not to grocery shop with Robin, who mischievously tossed things like cookies and nacho-flavored Doritos into the shopping cart while she wasn't looking, like a kid. Standing in the cookie aisle, Teresa felt a sudden pang of loneliness and bought some Mint Milanos, Robin's favorites, just to have her close.

From the street she saw the light on in her living room, and was both pleased and annoyed when Robin greeted her at the door.

"Surprise!" Robin sang out, but she must have noticed something in Teresa's face. "Donald canceled on me to get laid. Gay *boys*. So I decided to surprise you. That's okay, right?"

"Oh, honey, sure," Teresa said, smiling and handing her the grocery bag. "Any time. You know that. That's why you have keys." She saw her evening alone melt around her. They would fix dinner together, talk, clean up, go to bed, read for ten minutes, not have sex, not talk about it, fall asleep. Teresa had been trying to get through the novel *Beloved* in ten-minute intervals for months. She had imagined herself in the bathtub with it, reading languidly for an hour while bubbles popped around her.

"Something's wrong," Robin observed as Teresa pushed past her into the kitchen and got each of them a Rolling Rock.

"Not at all," Teresa said unconvincingly. "Look, I got everything for lemon chicken. And I even picked up Mint Milanos. Somehow, I must have known you were going to be here!"

Robin leaned against the door frame swigging her beer and eyeing Teresa as she unpacked the groceries. Teresa dropped a lemon self-consciously and it rolled under the sink.

"What?" Teresa asked anxiously. "What are you staring at?"

"You," Robin answered. "You don't want me here, do you? You're disappointed I came. I *know* you."

"Robin," Teresa said, exasperated and guilty at the same time, "that's not true." When she said it, she meant it wasn't true that she was disappointed, but it sounded more like she thought it wasn't true that Robin knew her.

"Okay, maybe I don't know you at all," Robin said, much too loudly. "You're so fucking distant sometimes, who *could* know you?"

Teresa looked at her sadly. It was not the first time a lover had called her distant. They had each, in their own way, expressed the same concern, and their chorus of observations echoed in her brain.

"Don't hold yourself back, babe," Andrew chided. "I want to see the real you."

"You really clam up sometimes," Matthew noted.

"You're somewhere else, aren't you?" Roz mused.

"What's going on in there?" Dana asked, tapping Teresa's forehead lightly. "Earth to Teresa."

When it came down to it, Robin had hit a soft spot. Being alone always felt more natural to Teresa than being coupled. Standing in the kitchen, clutching a package of chicken cutlets, Teresa began to cry, her chest heaving, her breaths coming in watery gulps. Robin removed the chicken from her hands and laid it on the counter. Finally, Teresa was sobbing onto her shoulder. "It's okay, baby," Robin whispered soothingly into her ear, her lips stiff against Teresa's neck. "It's okay."

. . .

"FEEL THIS," Tom said, "would you?"

He had a hand on the right side of his throat, which he extended toward her.

"Does this feel swollen to you, the gland?"

Teresa's fingers caressed the knob in his neck, a marble under the skin. She pushed at it, trying to press it back into the flesh.

"Ouch," he complained. "Not so hard. Did you feel it?"

"Yes," she said, her hand falling back into her lap at the dinner table. "Yes, it feels swollen."

"I thought so." He resumed his meal, which he had painstakingly prepared for the two of them. It was the eve of the Lesbian and Gay Pride March, and neither one of them was in the mood for a parade just weeks after Jamie's death.

"Come to the Lesbian Pride Dance," Gloria had urged. "It'll take your mind off things."

"I can't," Teresa said helplessly. "I . . . promised Tom." What she didn't say was that the thought of trying to have a good time with Jamie dead was too painful.

Tom fixed broiled swordfish with arugula and tomato salad. The arugula was so spicy it burned her throat, but the discomfort was somehow just what she wanted. "All this damn pollen, I can't stand it," he went on. "My glands can't stand it."

She let her eyes brim with tears, blaming the arugula. She couldn't find the right words to ask, so the wrong, insufficient ones came out instead.

"Tom, are you okay? I mean, are you *okay?*"

He glanced up at her. He couldn't have missed the tears, which weighted down her lashes.

"Tell me," she said, her words like echoes in her ears.

He was quiet a long time, then took a noisy swallow of Chardonnay and licked it from his lips thoughtfully.

"Teresa, I . . . I haven't been tested," he began slowly. "Before you say anything, let me finish. I know this might be hard for you to understand, but I don't want to be. I don't want to live knowing. Jamie and I discussed it, we both knew we were pretty high risk. And now I figure, chances are with Jamie gone I've got it, too, and until something happens to me I'd rather just not know."

You fucker, she thought, but she meant Jamie. Once, afraid to ask Tom himself, she questioned Jamie about Tom's health. He said Tom was "fine," and she assumed that meant negative. But what did "fine" mean; whose idea of "fine" was he? And now he had a marble in his neck that he was willing to chalk up to allergies but obviously concerned about just the same.

So that's the way it would be.

"Fine," she said, stuffing an unmanageable leaf into her mouth. It was not really Tom's decision she didn't accept, but the whole epidemic. "That's just fine," she said again, defeatedly.

. . .

NOT LONG after Jamie died, Teresa ran into Dana, her ex-lover, on the street. She was holding hands with a slim man with intellectual-looking round glasses. Spotting Teresa, Dana dropped his hand like it was a raw wire.

"Teresa," she said sheepishly. Her companion looked confused by the sudden abandonment.

"Dana Wright," Teresa said, as if there were other

Danas in her past, as if she had to hone her memory, which was already as sharp as a knife. "I haven't seen you in . . . too long, I guess."

"Three years, I think," Dana mused, edging slightly away from the man; dissociating herself? "Are you and Robin still together?"

"No," Teresa answered, "that's been over for about two years. She couldn't take her eyes from the blue shirt-front of the slim man, but she was too nervous to look him directly in the eyes. And since Dana wasn't introducing him, there seemed to be no call to look up that far. Yet her curiosity was piqued, and her first thought was that she had to rush home and call Jamie with the dish.

Then she remembered he was dead.

"How are you, Dana?" Teresa asked, at the same time meeting the man's eyes. They were a foamy green color behind the gray frames of his glasses. The effect was disconcerting, like staring through green bottle glass at close range. "What have you been up to?"

"This is S-sam," Dana sputtered, as if she'd forgotten his name or possibly would have liked to. "We met working on Jesse Jackson's campaign."

Sam extended his hand shyly. Teresa took it in hers, surprised and amused to find her handshake firmer than his.

"This is Teresa," Dana finished, as if that said it all.

Dana was the last person Teresa would have ever expected to find with a male lover. When they were together years before, Dana labeled herself a "pure lesbian" because she had scrupulously avoided ever having sex with men.

"Does that make me an 'impure lesbian'?" Teresa laughed. "Or just a tarnished one?"

"You are definitely spoiled goods," Dana joked, "and I may ruin my reputation just speaking to you."

They had trashed lesbians they knew who started dating

men. "Mary Carr's sleeping with a man," Dana announced. "Before that it was Pauline Chang. Is this some sort of epidemic or what?"

"It's a nightmare," Teresa agreed.

"Worse than that, Mary's calling herself 'bisexual.' Like she's scared of the 'S' word. Bisexual—what the fuck is that?" Dana asked with real venom. "I mean, shit or get off the pot."

When they were lovers, Dana refused to penetrate Teresa in any way or with any thing.

"You don't need penetration in sex," Dana chastised her when in the throes of passion Teresa had asked for her fingers. "You just think you do." Teresa wanted to say, "No, I don't need it, but I like it," but because that didn't seem like a permissible thought, she kept it to herself. After all, Dana had spent years in the women's movement, hammering out her political analysis. Compared to her, Teresa was a neophyte feminist who had never even made it all the way through *Sexual Politics* or *The Second Sex*. During their relationship, Teresa kept a lot of things to herself: that she questioned Dana's intolerance of S/M; that she couldn't support her anti-porn stance; that she didn't think separatism was viable; that she sometimes fantasized about men. Now, still staring almost rudely at Sam, Teresa wondered if Dana had fantasized about men, too, but hadn't felt free enough to admit it. There were too many things people didn't or couldn't say to each other, she thought. What hadn't she said to Jamie?

"My uncle Jamie died," Teresa said when there was a pause in the conversation. They'd briefly talked of Dana's legal aid job, Teresa's writing. "You remember him?"

"Sure. I read the obit in the *Times*," Dana said, apparently not ashamed to admit that she hadn't called or even sent a note. "I'm so sorry."

"Yes, thanks," Teresa muttered, wanting suddenly to end the meeting, to turn and walk off and cry. All the cards she'd sent to Jamie's friends who lost lovers and best friends; all the contributions made in their names—how many had there been? Most of the men Teresa hardly knew, but she'd done it because it was what was done. Yet her ex-lover unabashedly admitted that she hadn't taken the time to pick up a pen, the phone. When did everything come to this, and why did she have such lousy taste in lovers?

"Well, take care," Teresa said, with a half-hearted yet gracious smile. An image crossed her mind as she brushed Dana's cheek with her own. It was of Dana holding her in her arms in a sliver of moonlight the first night they had sex. The moon crossed their four breasts like a thin spotlight. Then it moved.

"It was nice to meet you," Sam said politely.

"Are you still in the book?" Dana asked. "I'll call you, we'll have a drink."

"Still on Fifteenth Street," Teresa smiled. "Almost fourteen years." She knew Dana would never phone, and she realized sadly that she didn't mind.

"Good luck," Dana called, though with what, Teresa wasn't clear. Her writing? Her love life? Her grief?

"You, too," she answered, meaning specifically with Sam. It was good to need someone, woman or man, and Dana had always craved companionship. As she watched them walk off, rejoining hands, Teresa thought maybe it wasn't such good dish after all.

* * *

ROBIN GOT a cream vellum envelope in the mail addressed to her and Teresa. It was hand lettered with a black calligraphy pen.

Melinda Stein and Alanna Wilson
invite you
to a celebration of their commitment

"I hear they're both wearing tuxes," Robin observed. "One white and one black, just like them. But Alanna's wearing the white one and Melinda the black. What a pisser, huh?"

Teresa smiled over her bagel and coffee. She knew it was all the rage for gay people to get "married"—"commit themselves," Gloria liked to joke—but something about it made Teresa nervous. One by one, the lesbian couples she knew were sporting gold rings on their right hands, moving to New Jersey and Long Island. Alanna and Melinda wanted two kids and a Toyota.

Teresa couldn't recall ever wanting to be married, though her mother had tried to prime her for it. Alison had once told her she'd have to change her name when she got married, and the idea was unappealing. They had both had all the requisite home-making toys—a child-sized kitchen, a mini vacuum cleaner, a bassinet for their many baby dolls. When she graduated from college, Teresa was expecting a watch or a fountain pen as a present from her parents, but instead, the large Gimbel's box enclosed eight French crystal wine glasses.

"Oh," Teresa said, thinking how she'd gotten accustomed to drinking Paul Masson wine from juice glasses stolen from the school cafeteria. She had a set of six. "What are these for?"

"For your hope chest," her mother beamed. "I never had wine glasses, and I always wanted them." It could not have been an inexpensive gift, but Teresa was ungracious anyway.

"I didn't just get engaged, I graduated from college," she frowned.

"And you'll be getting married soon enough, I'm sure,"

her mother said cheerfully. "That nice boy Matthew can't take his eyes off you." She nodded casually in the direction of a tall, angular young man with a long face, and Teresa looked away without even acknowledging him, even though they'd slept together two or three times.

"No weddings for me if I can help it," Teresa snapped, shutting the box lid over the glasses. There was a crease of pain in her mother's forehead that Teresa took some pleasure in.

"The commitment's two weeks from Sunday," Robin noted, rereading the invitation. "What should we get them?"

"An appointment with a couples' counselor? No, I'm kidding," Teresa said quickly when the joke fell flat. "You know them better than I do, Rob."

"I know—there's this shop near work that sells gorgeous Indian cloth. I could get some for a tablecloth. How does that sound?"

Teresa nodded. "Fine, I guess. As long as they have a table." Neither she nor Robin nor most of their friends had apartments big enough to accommodate tables.

Robin smiled and folded the invitation into its envelope thoughtfully. "What do you think of all this marriage stuff?" she asked. "I mean, do you ever want to get married?"

Part of Teresa longed to be tied to someone forever, to trust she'd never lose her, to have the ring to prove it. Sometimes she thought she could have that with Robin. But the other part of her warred against it. It was hard to imagine a joint checking account, a shared apartment, someone who never went *home*. When she met Robin, Teresa had lived ten years on Fifteenth Street by herself. It was not without careful consideration that she'd cleared a dresser drawer for Robin and bought some extra hangers for the closet. If they moved in together, they'd have to get a bigger place, since neither her apartment nor Robin's postage-stamp-sized studio would serve.

"It's hard to imagine being married," Teresa said. "I mean, most of my life I've just felt . . . well, like one person."

"You *are* one person," Robin snapped, wrinkling her forehead. "What's that supposed to mean?"

"I know. It's too hard to explain. I've just been alone so long, I've gotten used to it. It feels like the natural state."

Robin bit into her bagel and chewed it methodically. "So you'd probably never marry, say, me."

Teresa panicked—had she said that? She squeezed Robin's hand reassuringly on the table. "I didn't say that. I said marriage is hard to imagine, not that I wouldn't do it. There's a difference."

"Is there?" Robin asked.

At Melinda and Alanna's commitment, Teresa softened to the idea of union. The couple was joined by two friends: a Jewish gay male stand-up comic who dressed like a rabbi for the occasion, and an African-American lesbian poet who wrote a special wedding verse. When Melinda crushed the glass and the guests shouted "Mazel tov!" a chill ran up Teresa's back.

"It's so romantic," she sighed, taking Robin's arm. "It makes me want to break into that sappy song, you know— 'Is there a canopy in store for me?'"

Robin grinned with the memory of a good story. "There was this seder at my bubbe's when I was about thirteen, and my cousin Marty brought his girlfriend. People kept asking him when they were getting married, and Marty finally announced that they were planning to move in together instead. The room was teeming with relatives, and it got really quiet. All of a sudden, my bubbe called out from the corner, 'No chuppa, no shtup-a!' I think Bubbe saying 'shtup' was a bigger shock for everyone than Marty doing it!"

Teresa laughed, though she wished the conversation had

stayed serious. "Maybe marriage wouldn't be so scary after all," she ventured, imagining Robin breaking the glass at their own ceremony. Would her parents come? Alanna's mother and sister had sniffled through the entire ceremony. In Teresa's case, she wasn't sure if her mother would disapprove more of the lesbian part or the Jewish part. "Wouldn't it be funny to be, you know, engaged?"

Robin smiled her polite smile, the one she reserved for Teresa's least appealing suggestions. "Yeah, it would be funny." Robin scanned the crowd of guests, mostly lesbians. "It's hard to imagine, really, with all these lesbians, saying 'forever and ever' to one woman. I mean, how could you ever be sure?"

It must have been then that Teresa knew Robin would leave. She just couldn't admit she'd ever guessed it.

. . .

ROBIN LEFT on a Tuesday, and the next evening Gloria came over to help Teresa with the job of clearing out Robin's things. Though they'd never lived together, Robin's possessions had accumulated over time at Teresa's. Tuesday morning, Robin merely grabbed her camera, which was lying out on Teresa's desk. "I'll come back later for the rest," she said; but the thought of Robin spending hours in the apartment sorting out her possessions was more than Teresa could stand.

"I'll do it," Teresa insisted. "I'll put all your stuff in boxes and you can just pick them up when I'm not here. And we'll do the same with the things I have at your place."

It meant sorting mostly through clothes. Half of Robin's wardrobe had ended up at Teresa's. It also meant some books, computer disks, and odds and ends, like a Scrabble game and a cast-iron skillet. Removing the clothes left more room in Teresa's closet and drawers than she remembered having.

"You should fix her and take all this stuff over to Astor Place and sell it," Gloria suggested as they loaded shirts and pants into a garbage bag. "Maybe you could get, what, ten bucks? God, this girl had bad taste." Gloria picked out a plaid shirt from the pile with disapproval.

"That's actually mine," Teresa grinned, "but she bought it for me."

"You're giving back a present?" Gloria asked, shocked but impressed, too. "That takes balls."

There were sentimental things that made Teresa's eyes mist over. A ring and a bracelet she'd given Robin for Hanukkah, a book of Audre Lorde's poetry she'd bought early on in their relationship and inscribed, "I've never been so in love—Teresa." A Valentine card Teresa had made and Robin had framed. By the end of the evening, Teresa felt like an empty box.

"Do you want me to spend the night?" Gloria asked as she taped the final carton shut. But Teresa just wanted to be alone. She'd been holding back a good cry all night, afraid that the ferocity of it might alarm Gloria. The second the door closed after her friend, the tears streamed down Teresa's cheeks, and she cried until her head ached. Then she crawled into bed at ten o'clock and cried herself to sleep.

Her dreams were all of Robin. In one, Robin didn't recognize her on the street. In another (or maybe it was the same dream?) Robin and her new girlfriend had sex in the middle of Teresa's living room. In the last installment, Robin confessed to Teresa's mother that she had never loved Teresa at all, she just pretended. Teresa's mother admitted she'd done the same thing for years.

"Is it too late to call? You said I could call," Teresa said. "I could call back tomorrow if it's too late." It was long after midnight and Gloria sounded groggy.

"Teresa, it's fine. Besides, it *is* tomorrow."

They talked for twenty minutes, or rather Teresa talked

and cried and Gloria listened, inserting a reassuring "Uh-huh" or "It's hard" every now and then.

"I *lose* people," Teresa sobbed. "I get attached to them and then they go away."

"I'm not going anywhere. Jamie and Tom aren't going anywhere," Gloria observed. "You have people who really care about you who are in it for the long haul. You're not *doing* anything to lose people."

Teresa felt calmer. Her heart slowed down to a normal speed. "You're right," she said. "I'm just not used to sleeping alone. I keep thinking I hear Robin's footsteps in the hall. I'll get used to it again."

They said good night, and Teresa lay awake in the dark listening to the sounds of Fifteenth Street. A trash can lid being rattled, an EMS car on its way to St. Vincent's Hospital, a duet of barking dogs, a singing drunk. She was glad the worst was over, that Robin's things soon would be gone from sight.

"You just need some time to mourn, really," Gloria had advised, and Teresa had found that a funny way to phrase it. "It could take months."

Friday evening she did her laundry. It was a way of avoiding the fact that almost every Friday for two years she'd been with Robin. Only last Friday they'd gone to the movies, had dinner out, came home and tried to have sex. Tried, but fell asleep in the middle, blaming the dinner wine and ignoring the truth.

Mixed in with her underwear and jeans in the laundry bag was Robin's Pep Boys tee-shirt, a classic from a Delaware auto parts store, which featured the smiling cartoon faces of Manny, Moe and Jack—the Pep Boys. It was one of Robin's favorites and a shirt Teresa had always coveted.

She washed it with her light things and carried it home, neatly folded, fully intending to place it in the bag with the other clothes for Robin to pick up. In fact, Teresa did put it in there. But the next morning she retrieved it from the pile and hid it in a drawer until after Robin took her things away. Then little by little—first around the apartment, then out on the street—she began to wear it.

. . .

SURPRISINGLY, after Robin left, Teresa felt not only devastated but relieved.

The relief didn't come right away. She noticed it several weeks later when she was leafing through take-out menus after work, deciding what dinner food to order in. The most frequently consulted menus were stuffed into the front of the Manhattan yellow pages. Teresa sorted through Chinese, Indian, Japanese, Mexican, and Italian, but then she remembered something. There was a smaller stack of menus in the desk drawer near the phone that she had hardly looked at since she'd been with Robin. Middle Eastern, Thai—the foods Robin hated and didn't want Teresa to order when they were together because they couldn't share. At first Teresa was so in love she could easily sublimate any desire to Robin's. Later, as the relationship ebbed, she found she really had a taste for Pad Thai.

The menus were so old most of the entrees had increased in price by two or three dollars. Without thinking, Teresa ordered spring rolls, coconut milk soup, Pad Thai and Chicken Musaman from her favorite Thai restaurant. Enough for two. Then she gorged herself in front of Peter Jennings and the ABC Evening News.

But that was what Robin watched, the only TV she permitted herself. Robin carried on a running commentary.

"I can't believe this is where Americans get their information. Did you hear what they said about AIDS funding?"

"Why can't he say 'gay' instead of 'homosexual'? These newscasters drive me *crazy.*"

At the end of the broadcast, just as the music for *Jeopardy* was beginning, Robin would click off the set.

"Right from world events into game shows," she would say. "Ah, the American mind."

Teresa thought about that as the familiar music played. She thought, television rots your mind, and it's too depressing to watch *Jeopardy* while eating dinner alone. But then she gave herself five minutes. Ten. Just until Double Jeopardy. Until Final Jeopardy.

"Who are Toni Morrison and Alice Walker?" she screamed at the set. The three white male contestants couldn't dredge up the question for the answer, "Two black women writers who won the Pulitzer Prize."

"Pathetic," Teresa said aloud, getting up to click off the television. She felt a momentary twinge of guilt at enjoying the game show, then stuffed a tiny spring roll into her mouth.

Jamie called a few minutes later. He was home from the hospital but recuperating in front of the TV. "You're not going to believe this," he said, "but tonight on *Jeopardy* one of the questions was about Toni Morrison and Alice Walker."

She thought of saying, "Yeah, I watched it," but Robin was still too much present. Teresa had just found her Pep Boys tee shirt in the laundry bag, an errant sock under the bed.

"No kidding," she replied. She popped another spring roll into her mouth, but by then it was cold and left an unpleasant taste.

. . .

AMONG OTHER things, Jamie suffered from CMV retinitis at the end, which made him go almost blind. In Jamie's last weeks, Teresa came to the apartment to read to him every night and to give Tom time to himself. She no longer had any other life she cared about, apart from Jamie and Tom.

"You should take some time off for good behavior," Jamie quipped, "and see your friends."

"You *are* my friends."

"I mean your other friends. Gloria, for one."

"She understands," Teresa said, but she knew that Gloria really didn't. Gloria left messages asking her to *do* things—have dinner, go to parties, bowl—as if her life could go one while Jamie's was ending. Teresa knew her friend didn't understand how close that end was for Jamie, but she found it impossible to pick up the phone and say the words that would explain her withdrawal. Each time she thought of calling Gloria, her fingers dialed Jamie and Tom instead.

Teresa opened *The Plague* carefully so the binding didn't crack. Her books always appeared to be fresh from the bookstore, even if she'd read them several times.

Jamie had requested a diet of the less famous novels of great writers, and they were slow to read aloud. They had plowed through the entire *Mill on the Floss* and *Sister Carrie* before he asked for Camus.

"I can't believe I never read it," he said with an embarrassed shake of his head. "I think it's a book I should read before I die."

Teresa had never really read Camus either, except *L'Etranger* in her French course requirement at Fordham. She had missed a lot of the meaning because her vocabulary wasn't very good, and she had to keep stopping to look up words in Larousse.

"'You must picture the consternation of our little town, hitherto so tranquil, and now, out of the blue, shaken to its core, like a quite healthy man who all of a sudden feels his temperature shoot up and the blood seething like wildfire in his veins,'" she read aloud, each word weighted with significance. Every so often, she glanced up at Jamie to catch his expression. His lips were slightly parted, and he seemed to drink in every word. He rubbed his fingers together on the sheet, itching to hold the book himself. She had never known Jamie to be without some sort of reading material, wherever he happened to be.

Teresa's parents had always made sure she had plenty of books, and they had read to Alison and her when they were children. But Teresa had never seen either of them buy a book for themselves or check one out of the library. Jamie was the one who got her her first library card at the main branch of Carnegie Public Library in Pittsburgh. He had escorted her and Alison one Saturday, and they each got pink cards with their names printed on them that permitted them ten books from the Children's Room. Jamie's card was white and allowed him a limitless number of books at a time.

"Could you take out twenty?" nine-year-old Alison had asked in wonder.

"If I wanted," he replied.

"How about fifty?" she pursued.

"You bet."

"How about fifty million?" Teresa asked eagerly, and she and Alison exploded into giggles.

"They don't have that many books," Jamie smiled slyly, "but if they did, I could have them *all*."

"Do you think someone could read all the books in the library in their life?" Alison asked, sobering.

"I don't know about you," Jamie winked, "but I plan to."

Somewhere in the last few paragraphs, Jamie's fingers stopped twitching on the bed and his breath became a shallow snore. Teresa marked the place in the book, dimmed the light, and backed quietly toward the door. In the frame she stood and watched him sleep for several moments, double-checking for the subtle rise and fall of his chest that indicated life.

* * *

A CARD from Gloria arrived in the mail, a Lichtenstein-like cartoon on the front of a woman holding her head and saying, "I can't believe I forgot to have children!" Inside Gloria had placed a stamped postcard for reply.

"Teresa," the card read, "Are you okay? I'm worried about you, girlfriend! What's happening with Jamie? Why don't you call me? Please check off one of the options on the enclosed card. Con cariño, Gloria."

Gloria had typed a list on the stamped postcard.

Dear Gloria,
[   ] I'm fine, just busy, don't worry.
[   ] I've been better, don't worry yet.
[   ] I've never been worse, worry all you want.
[   ] Other: _____
XXOO,

Teresa smiled and pulled out a pen to check "other" and write a message, but at the last moment checked all four available boxes. "Life (and death) are confusing and hard," she wrote on the blank line. "Thanks for caring."

Though Gloria would understand the message, it still wouldn't be enough, Teresa knew. It would frustrate Gloria, whose hands-on friendship had always appealed to Teresa but which now was more than she could handle. She didn't want to talk about Jamie's illness with anyone. It was bad enough that she had to watch it, day after day.

. . .

"WHAT DID you do with all of it?" Jamie asked. "Do you have it in New York?" He had returned to the hospital to die and was most lucid in the early mornings. Teresa arrived every day at seven-thirty and stayed for an hour before rushing off to work. Then she returned in the evenings to say good night or read aloud, never sure which would be the last time.

"All of what?" she said, thinking his mind was starting to fade earlier and earlier in the day.

"All of your writing," he explained. They hadn't been discussing it, though Tom had mentioned a gay friend's story he'd recently read in *The New Yorker*, and Teresa had commented bitterly that mainstream magazines found gay male writers more palatable than lesbian. "From when you were little," he finished. "You had a character you called Carla Something. You let me read a few of the stories once."

"Carla Carlotta," Teresa said with a little smile. "My alter ego."

Tom looked up curiously from his coffee mug, which read in black letters across the front, "There's more to life than coffee... but don't ask me *what*." He bought it in the hospital gift shop because he couldn't stand the cafeteria's styrofoam take-out cups. In his anxiety he tended to nibble on them and get splinters of foam in his coffee.

"When I went away to college," Teresa continued, "I left all my stories in a box in my closet at home. I don't know what happened to them. Once when I was in Pittsburgh I asked Mom about the box, and we looked but couldn't find it. She must have accidentally tossed it out. You know how she likes to clean." Teresa didn't add that she had actually forgotten all about the box until Robin asked if she had saved her early writings.

Tom studied the contents of his mug, and Jamie's eyes closed briefly. "All of it's gone?" Jamie asked, perhaps hoping for the one story that had slipped through the pile to safety.

"Every last bit," she said firmly, trying to convince herself it was without sadness. She watched as he shifted his body an inch or two with great effort, refusing Tom's offer of help.

"And I thought *my* life was a tragedy," Jamie said, shaking his head.

Tom fished a coffee grain from his mug with the tip of his thumb. He pondered it briefly, then rubbed it off onto his jeans. "That doesn't happen anymore, does it?" he asked slowly. "I mean, you're careful with your writing now, aren't you?"

"Well," she said, "it was a bad habit to break. I actually don't have anything I wrote before 1983." Tom winced.

Now she kept back-up files of all her work and stored duplicate hard copies of all her unpublished writing in the freezer. There was nothing else in there, not even an ice cube tray. A friend had advised her that without a metal strong box, the freezer was the next best thing—it wouldn't burn in a fire. Of course, it made for warm drinks on hot days and no ice cream, but then it was a forty-year-old Coldspot that let ice cream go runny anyway.

"I would have loved to have you read me those stories," Jamie sighed. "You were quite a kid."

He dozed off before she got a chance to ask him what he meant.

Tom invited her to the cafeteria for breakfast. "Some powdered eggs and toast with margarine?" he suggested.

"Got to go do inch counts," she said, declining, and sorry that she had to. He had been particularly pensive all morning, like he felt the imminence of Jamie's leaving.

"Ooh, inch counts," he said, with forced gaiety.

She smiled, spontaneously grabbed his hand, and uncharacteristically for her, pressed it to her mouth and kissed it lightly, just grazing the skin.

Tom reddened and quickly took her hand in his. "This is how Jamie does it," he said, lifting her hand to kiss but kissing his own instead.

"Of course he does," she smiled. "He's a man."

. . .

HER MOTHER cried at the airport, full-fledged sobbing that made other travelers and their entourages stare at her with concern. Teresa's father wrapped an arm around his wife, looking a little embarrassed at her display of emotion. Her mother blew her nose noisily into a small handkerchief with a gardenia print on it.

"Are you sure you want to go through with this?"

Teresa's eyes filled with tears at the sight of her mother in so much pain. She bit her lips and blinked hard to fight the tears back.

"Mom," she said softly, "we've been through this a million times. Fordham's the best choice for me." She dug her thumbs into the waist of her jeans, which rode below her hip bones. The pants gripped her thighs then flared into enormous bell-bottoms that dragged on the ground. The ends were badly frayed, and long strings of denim trailed out behind her. Her mother, who always dressed up to travel, had argued with her about wearing the jeans on the plane, but Teresa had defiantly insisted.

"I *have* to be wearing jeans when I get there," she maintained. "I just have to." She knew that it would never do to appear at college the first day wearing her mini-skirted graduation dress with stockings, as her mother had proposed. First impressions were everything.

Teresa hugged her father, who remained stiff and formal, unused to affection. He had never been big on physical contact, unlike Jamie, who was always touching or squeezing her. "Call if you need money," he instructed.

Her mother grabbed her as if she wouldn't let go. Her crying echoed in Teresa's ear.

"Mom," Teresa reminded her, "they've called the flight."

With her mother's tears still wet on her tee-shirt, Teresa disappeared through the loading ramp, smiling over her shoulder. Her own tears evaporated as she took her window seat and stared out at the terminal. Through the smoky glass of the terminal windows she could not find her parents, though she imagined her mother still sobbing. Dispelling the picture, Teresa dug into her backpack for the Fordham catalog.

"Journalism's a good field," Jamie had said a few evenings before on the phone. They were finalizing their plans to meet at La Guardia Airport. "Just don't stop writing stories, okay? The ones about Carla? I love those."

"Oh, there's no career in stories like that," she said quickly. "Mom read an article that said the average novelist earns about two thousand a year, if he's lucky. You can't live on that. It's just a hobby."

So without more discussion she boxed up all her childhood writing—stories, essays, notebooks of short novels, including the latest, the one she'd finished that summer. In it, Carla became a stringer for a newspaper and helped solve her own sister's murder.

Teresa's writing since the age of nine made a stack about a foot tall, a disappointing height, far less than she would have guessed. Most of it was about Carla Carlotta, who had grown up right along with her creator but now felt like a childhood friend Teresa needed to leave behind. Teresa stowed the box away in the back of her closet and stood peering in at it for several minutes before she closed the door.

"Are you going to Fordham?" asked the young man seated next to her. He was a blond jock with a tan that was too deep. The last thing she wanted to do was have a conversation with this boy, the type she and her friends had made fun of in high school, the stereotypical athlete with the straight "D" average. Her own crowd of friends, girls and boys, were the newspaper and yearbook staffs, writers and artists, who were all headed to scholarships at schools like

Georgetown and Notre Dame.

"Yeah," she answered, as briefly as she could, but the jock persisted.

"Me, too," he said. "I saw your catalog. I'm a sophomore. You a freshman?"

"Yeah," she said again.

"It's a great school," he enthused, flashing a white smile that suggested a recent trip to the dentist. Handsome as he was, he would never be someone she was attracted to. The few boys she had dated were all pale and thin with thoughtful eyes, boys who didn't drink or smoke and who shook her father's hand when they picked her up at the house, boys who came to the door and didn't honk rudely from the driveway, boys who kissed her demurely on the cheek, as if she were an aunt or grandmother, boys who tended to act like her girlfriends. The nicest of them all was Doug Shay, a courteous, earnest boy who had foresworn the debating team to perform poetry readings in interscholastic speech competitions. He'd won four trophies in city-wide tournaments for what the judges called "oral interpretation." His prize-winning recitation was taken from *Leaves of Grass*.

"You'll love Fordham," the blond jock continued. How did *he* know, when he'd just met her? She forced a smile and returned to her list of journalism courses.

"I'm Dan," he offered, his arm pressing slightly against hers on the arm rest, simply because it could. She looked up again and into his blue eyes as the plane taxied away from the terminal. She threw one last look toward where her family would still be standing behind the gray windows.

"I'm Teresa," she introduced herself, turning back to him. But that didn't quite say who she was now that she was an adult and headed off to college. "Teresa Keenan," she added, just to listen to the sound of the words in her mouth.

. . .

TERESA KNEW her mother's handwriting from all the years of being excused from school for colds, flu, fever, menstrual cramps. "Please excuse Teresa Keenan from school yesterday, as she had _____ ." The precisely rounded writing resembled the examples in Teresa's Palmer Method handwriting manual when she was seven.

But it was odd to see it on an envelope, with the return address in Pittsburgh seeming even farther away than the five hundred miles it actually was.

> *Miss Teresa Frances Keenan*
> *Fordham University*
> *Box 754*
> *Bronx, New York 10468*

She would have to tell her mother a few things: She had always hated the "Frances" part of her name, that's why she didn't use it, and the "Miss" would have to go. Women were now opting to be called "Ms."; there was even a new magazine with that title, devoted to feminist issues. Teresa knew that neither of these revelations would make the slightest impression on her mother. Trying to express her ideas with her was like trying to talk with laryngitis.

There was no other mail in the box for Teresa except an advertisement for a credit card. She ripped open her mother's envelope, which had a colorful fall cascade of pumpkins and maple leaves across the front. Teresa had never seen the stationery before, and figured her mother had just bought it. But the paper inside didn't match. Her mother had written the letter on light purple paper with a vague hint of scent that Teresa couldn't place.

"Dear Teresa," the letter began. "How's this for funny stationery? I guess you can tell I don't write letters very often, because I only had these odds and ends from who knows when. I will have to get something better so I can write you a

<u>nice</u> letter." Throughout, her mother sprinkled underlining for emphasis.

> *How are you? I'm fine. Your father had a little cold last week, but now seems to be fine, too. It is <u>quiet</u> around here without you!*
>
> *How is school? Are you glad you went to Fordham instead of to Pitt? "The Bronx" seems like it might be an awful place, but your uncle tells us you're in the <u>north</u> Bronx not the <u>south</u> Bronx, so I guess that's OK.*
>
> *I'm sending you some newspaper clippings that I thought you might be interested in. I thought you'd like to know that Sr. Mary Bernard, your principal at St. Sebastian's, celebrated fifty years in the order last week. Your father and I sent some roses to the convent, I thought she'd like that, and I'm <u>amazed</u> that in this day and age any nun could keep her vocation for so long. Most of the young sisters who taught at St. Sebastian's have left the order. I don't think I ever told you this, but if something should happen to your father, I think I would go off to a convent. He says the same thing, that he'd go to a monastery.*

Teresa skipped the article but noted the difference in Sr. Mary Bernard's style since grade school days. Then, she had worn a stiff white collar and headband with her hot, restrictive black habit. A heavy wooden cross clacked against the collar as she walked. Now, her curly gray hair peeked from beneath a short wimple, and her habit was visibly softer and less confining. She smiled broadly for the camera, showing perfect white teeth.

Teresa remembered the times she and Alison had spent discussing the nuns' hair and grooming habits.

"Sr. Felicity is *definitely* a blonde," Alison decided. "You can tell it by her light eyebrows. And Sr. Perpetua must be a redhead."

"Do they wash their hair?" Teresa wondered.

"Of course, they do," Alison scoffed. "But it doesn't get as dirty as ours under their veils. And they're not allowed to set it or anything. If a nun has straight hair and wants it to be curly, she can't do anything about it."

"You can't see it anyway," Teresa pointed out.

"Well...yeah," Alison admitted, caught in her own reasoning. "That's why. There wouldn't be any reason for it."

The second article Teresa's mother sent was the engagement announcement of a girl in Teresa's grade school class whom she hardly remembered. "Didn't Mary Kate grow up pretty?" her mother wrote, but Teresa knew it was a not-so-subtle nudge. "I don't know why you need college," her mother had admonished. "If you're like me, you'll be married when you've barely hit your twenties." How many times Teresa had longed to say, "But I'm not like you, Mom!"

The third article was a doctor's advice column about treating acne ("For when your face breaks out"), and the final one was about a tourist's harrowing experiences on a trip to New York ("Maybe you should carry your money in your sock when you go out?").

I hardly know how to cook anymore for just the two of us! I'm constantly fixing too much and having leftovers, and you know how your dad hates having the same meal twice in a week! So I try to turn them into something else, like making meat loaf sandwiches out of supper or a chicken casserole when there's roast chicken left over. I've been picking up Family Circle *magazine at the A&P because they give you lots of leftover recipes in there.*

There had been other times when supper got the best of her mother. After Alison died, there were always too many potatoes, green beans that didn't get eaten, meat left for the next day's lunch. Until she got accustomed to cutting back portions, Teresa's mother simply threw the extra food away and didn't worry about remaking it into another meal. It was almost as if she couldn't clear the table fast enough, couldn't wait to get rid of the unnecessary food, the mere sight of it too stinging a reminder.

I talked to your dad about my getting a little job, but he wasn't too keen on it. You know, just a few hours a week somewhere. Georgina's Gifts was looking for someone a while back, and I thought I'd like something like that. They give the salesgirls a <u>discount,</u> too. Your dad says I never had to work, why start now.

I might volunteer at the church instead. They need some office help, and I used to be a pretty good typist before I got married. Maybe I'll practice on a letter to you. Last week I was supposed to help out at the church's annual fall feast, but then your father was sick so I didn't go. Mrs. DeNardo said it was a nice event, but your dad needed me.

Well, I've got to go put the laundry in the dryer and start your father's supper so that's it for now. I hope you're OK and know what you're doing up there. Call us on the weekend, but remember what I told you: Call person-to-person and ask for Teresa, and then we'll know it's you and call back. OK?

Take care,
Mom

Teresa turned the sheet over, looking for more. She wasn't sure what the "more" would be, but she still checked.

On the way back to the dorm, she tossed the newspaper articles into a trash can, but the letter she stuffed into her jeans pocket. She held onto it for a week, letting it sit out on her desk with her name staring back at her, reminding her to call home as instructed. "My, my, Miss Teresa Frances Keenan," Liane teased her. "Would Miss Teresa Frances Keenan care to go to dinner now?"

When Teresa realized there was nothing in the letter she needed to remember, it went the way of the clippings.

* * *

THE BELL for 5A read "Burns" and not "Newley," and Teresa rang it with trepidation. A voice at the other end crackled "Yeah?"

"It's Teresa Keenan, I called about the share," Teresa shouted toward the speaker.

There was some static, then a fumbling sound, then the inner door buzzed and Teresa pushed her way into the dark first floor hallway. Take-out menus that had been shoved under the door littered the entrance, and she glanced at their names with interest as she stepped over them. She knew there was good, cheap food in the East Village from the times she and her friends had come down from Fordham for Indian or Ukrainian. But then most things would taste good to her now after four years of cafeteria food.

It was a long climb up, and a cheerful voice somewhere in the distance urged her on. "Keep coming," it called. "You're almost there." Then "You made it," the voice congratulated her as she hit the fifth floor landing. "These stairs keep me in shape."

The pleasant voice belonged to the smallest woman Teresa had ever met. She didn't even top five feet, and Teresa towered over her at only five-five. The woman had an appealing gamine quality, with a feathery haircut and a loose black shirt worn like a mini-dress over tights. Her cheeks bloomed with health.

"I'm Roz Newley," she smiled, holding out a tiny hand that got lost in Teresa's. "Teresa, right?"

"I wasn't sure this was the right place," Teresa admitted. "Your name isn't on the bell."

"Oh, yeah, nobody has their name on the bell in this building," Roz observed. "It's one big sublet."

Teresa stepped into the kitchen, noticing first the prominent old claw-foot bathtub there. She had heard such things were common in East Village walk-ups, but she was still startled by the sight. Roz acted nonchalant, like it didn't exist.

"So this is the kitchen, obviously, and the living room's right off it," she noted, leading Teresa into the next room, furnished with an old brown sleep sofa, some chairs with ripped seats and a bicycle. "This is where you'd sleep. I have a little room off the kitchen. You have to walk through it to get to the john."

Teresa stood looking around, the sparse seediness of the place depressing her. Then she turned and spotted an old wooden bookcase behind her, crammed to overflowing with worn paperbacks, a touch of life the rest of the apartment lacked.

"Your books," Teresa smiled with relief.

"Yeah, all my philosophy books," Roz said, "I just finished my graduate course work at NYU."

"No kidding. Doctorate?" Teresa asked, though Roz looked like a kid, maybe sixteen tops.

"No, Master's," Roz corrected, with a grin that suggested she was flattered by the mistake.

They sat on the brown sofa, whose upholstery was a scratchy synthetic. Roz offered Teresa a beer, but realized it was only noon when Teresa glanced at her watch. "I have insomnia, I was up half the night," Roz said. "It seems later to me than it actually is."

Teresa explained that she needed a share just for the summer, because in September she was moving into a place on West Fifteenth Street that her uncle had located for her. It was the apartment of one of his friends who was going to Europe indefinitely, possibly for good.

"I could spend the summer with Jamie," Teresa said, "but I'd rather be downtown on my own."

"Yeah, of course," Roz agreed. "Who would want to live with their uncle?" She laughed and pulled out a box of Gauloises. She took one herself, then offered them to Teresa, who accepted even though she didn't smoke.

"It's not that," Teresa said, leaning toward the match Roz held out. "He's cool. But he lives on West End near Eighty-sixth, and I'd rather be down here."

Teresa coughed as the harsh smoke hit her lungs. She had only smoked a couple of times before, both with Liane, both with filtered American cigarettes. And she hadn't smoked pot since Andrew.

"So you're interested then?" Roz asked. "Two months is fine with me. I expect to be gone from here in the fall anyway. When I wrap up my thesis."

"Where are you going?" Teresa coughed.

"Probably back to Chicago, where I'm from," Roz said with a frown. "Anywhere that's not here."

They puffed in silence, Teresa wanting to ask more but afraid to pry. Roz drew the smoke expertly into her lungs and kept glancing at her sideways, as if she would have liked to say more, too.

"It's seventy-five a month," Roz said finally. "The share."

"That's good."

"Is the room okay?"

"Sure," Teresa said quickly, her eyes darting around the

dismal space again. She could hang a few posters, add some color. It would be fine. She liked Roz, she seemed comfortable and familiar. But there was a hint of sadness somewhere under the surface, a secret to be unlocked.

"Oh, by the way," Roz added, stubbing out her cigarette, "I should tell you something. I'm a lesbian."

Teresa coughed again, this time from surprise. "Oh," she said. "Okay." She was thinking, what is it about me that attracts lesbian roommates?

"But I don't have a lover right now," Roz continued. "She split last week. Hence," she said with a slight smile, "the share."

"Oh," Teresa repeated. "And the insomnia, I guess?"

Roz smiled again, bigger this time, and pulled out another Gauloise. She tapped the ends of it onto the box, and Teresa felt a little chill run up her arms as she did it. She watched as Roz took the cigarette between her lips and lit it. There was, she realized, something very sexy about it.

"Can I bring my suitcase down tonight?" Teresa asked.

Roz squinted through the smoke. "Or sooner," she said in a way that sent another chill through Teresa. Already Teresa was imagining what it would be like to kiss those lips.

. . .

TERESA'S PARENTS had a lack of interest in her activities that increased over the years since she had come out to them. They almost never called her and never asked questions.

"What's it about?" Teresa complained to Gloria, when her friend confessed that her mother was also curiously phone-shy. "The not calling."

"I think my mother's afraid to catch me in the middle of sex," Gloria snickered. "As if I'd *answer* the goddamn phone if I was buried in someone's crotch. If I only had as much sex as Mama *thinks* I do! . . ."

Teresa's parents had never met any of her girlfriends,

except Roz briefly, and then without knowing that she and their daughter had spent the summer after Teresa's college graduation in carnal bliss. They had come to New York to see Teresa's new apartment and to bring some much-needed items from Pittsburgh—old pots, pans and dishes to outfit her kitchen, blankets and pillows for the bed Jamie and Tom bought her as a house-warming gift, scatter rugs for the wooden floors.

"That Roz," her mother commented after they met, "is an odd girl."

"In what way?" Teresa asked defensively. Roz had spent an hour helping to move Teresa's things crosstown from their East Village share to West Fifteenth Street.

"Her clothes, for one," her mother continued. "She looks like a leftover beatnik. And that apartment! Why is the bathtub in the kitchen?" she asked disdainfully, as if Roz had purposely put it there to be contrary or radical, as if bathtub placement defined a person's character.

Later, after she came out to them, Teresa threw out her lovers' names—Dana, Robin—but her parents never raised a single question. Statements like "Robin and I went to Cape Cod for vacation" were met with the same aversion as if she had announced, "Robin ate me out all night, and it felt so *good.*"

Once, between Dana and Robin, Teresa convinced them to come to New York for a summer weekend, against her mother's better judgment. She wanted to go to Disney World instead. "We're only coming," her mother said, "so your father can see Ellis Island before it closes for renovation. He's gotten it in his head to see where his father got off the boat from Ireland."

Three were too many people for Teresa's small apartment, and they stayed out sightseeing as much as possible to avoid tripping over each other. Her parents had never really been tourists in New York, so Teresa borrowed Jamie's car and chaffeured them around town. Her mother sat in the back seat, while her father clutched the dashboard every time Teresa switched lanes.

"You weave in and out too much," her father commented, as Teresa zigzagged down Broadway toward New York Harbor. "You're gonna get side-swiped."

"You have to drive offensively in New York," Teresa said. "There's no other choice."

Her father was quiet on the ferry to Ellis Island, contemplating his own father's journey. Before its renovation, Ellis Island was a decaying shell of dirt and cobwebs, a tattered ghost that eerily shadowed the harbor. Only an active imagination could picture what it had actually been like in its heydey, at the turn of the century when Jack Keenan had first seen it, stepping off the boat from Ireland with one satchel of belongings to his name.

"What made him go to Pittsburgh from here?" Teresa asked, as they stood with their park ranger guide in the Great Hall, dusty light streaming down on them through the massive windows.

"I don't know," her father admitted, looking embarrassed that he had never questioned his father's choice of city. "Friends, maybe? Work? I just don't know."

Her mother preferred the shopping mall at South Street Seaport to the squalor of Ellis Island. "I don't think it's as big as South Hills Village, though," she noted. "I don't think there are as many shops. Doesn't it seem smaller, Richard?"

They ate dinner in Chinatown at one of Teresa's favorite restaurants on Pell Street, which they entered by descending a flight of stairs from the street. "Where are you taking us?" her mother asked suspiciously, clutching the handrail.

"You'll love this place, Mom," Teresa assured her, wondering as she did if they shouldn't have ordered something safer, like a pizza at home, instead.

"I've never had Chinese food," her father mused, pondering the multi-paged menu, flipping back and forth nervously considering his choices. He seemed a little frightened of the variety. "What funny names—Moo Shu Pork! Do you see that, Eileen?"

Her mother studied the first two pages and then closed the menu defeatedly. "There's nothing here we can eat," she sighed, and Teresa felt a pang of both sympathy and anger. The sympathy won out, and Teresa took the matter firmly in hand.

"Let me order," she suggested. "Can I order for the table?"

"Oh, you might as well," her mother said. "But I don't think I'll eat anything."

Later, when they had cleaned their plates of Beef with Broccoli, Shrimp Lo Mein, and the Happy Family combination, Teresa said, "That wasn't so bad, was it? See what you've been missing all these years?" and her mother just smiled and sugared her tea, while her father nibbled on an orange wedge.

On Sunday her parents went to mass at St. Patrick's Cathedral, and Teresa stayed home. Neither one of them suggested she accompany them, and Teresa figured it was because she was a sinning lesbian. In fact, she would have never considered attending mass at the cathedral, even if pressed by her mother. Teresa's favorite part of the Gay Pride March in June was when the parade stopped in front of St. Pat's and marchers wagged their fingers at the intolerant Cardinal O'Connor's domain: "Shame! Shame! Shame!"

She knew that her mother prayed for her, because she had said so once years before. "I light a candle for you every week," her mother had admitted, and Teresa was too perturbed to ask why. She wished she could go and blow the candles out.

"She wants to save your soul," Jamie suggested. "She hopes God will make you straight, my child!"

"She thought I should keep dating Doug Shay from high school," Teresa noted. "In her mind, he was the boy for me, because he was so polite and trustworthy, 'a real gentleman,' she used to say. The ironic thing is, he never touched me because I'd bet big money that he's gay. He used to read Whitman poems in speech tournaments, for God's sake! I bet he's sucking cock even as we speak."

"All that reciting Whitman," Jamie smiled. "It does funny things to a boy."

"What a beautiful church that is!" her mother enthused after mass. "I bought postcards to send to Father Donohue and Mrs. DeNardo."

"I kept wondering how many people it holds," her father said, leafing through a guide book he had picked up at the church gift shop.

As an antidote to their Catholicism, Teresa led her un-suspecting parents to Christopher Street for lunch. They strolled past the Oscar Wilde Memorial Bookshop, past the site of the Stonewall rebellion in 1969, across Sheridan Square to the Riviera Restaurant, where parties of gay men sipped Bloody Marys with their western omelets.

"Everyone here," her mother commented approvingly, glancing around at the tables, "seems to be in such good shape."

It was a perverse pleasure, but Teresa took it anyway. She wanted to say, *This is my life, these people are gay, like me, like Jamie,* but the words, of course, couldn't come out. They lay on her tongue like a heavy film that got washed away with the first sip of coffee at lunch. It was one more subject the Keenan family couldn't broach if their lives depended on it.

. . .

TERESA HAD gotten accustomed to her limited fame. In lesbian and gay company, there was often someone to "ooh" and "ah" when she introduced herself.

"Teresa Keenan, the novelist? I've been waiting for your next book! Will it be another mystery?"

"I wanted to *marry* Magda Pike."

"Are you really Teresa Keenan? I can't wait to tell my lover I met you. He's your biggest fan."

On the subway home from Tom's apartment one evening, she had nothing to read and was forced to scan the overhead ads, from the serious to the absurd. "AIDS Is a Woman's Issue." "Hemorrhoids? Call 1-800-MD-TUSCH." When she tired of reading and re-reading them, she glanced at the book of the woman next to her. Coincidentally it was Teresa's second novel, the mystery. She chuckled as she spotted words so familiar she knew she'd written them.

The woman looked cautiously sideways, aware that Teresa was reading over her shoulder. "What's so funny?" she asked, curiosity rather than confrontation in her voice. It was as deep as a man's, but more sonorous, and it resonated through the car. Keeping a finger in her place, she directed the front cover toward Teresa. "Have you read this novel?"

"Yes," Teresa said, grinning. "I wrote it."

"Oh," the woman smiled, self-consciously running a hand over her close-cropped hair. It had touches of white sprinkled through the brown in a way that made her age indeterminate, anywhere from thirty-five to fifty. "Well, it's good. I don't read mysteries much, but I'm enjoying this one. Ellen's a likable character." She sounded almost surprised.

Tell me more, Teresa wanted to say, but didn't. Instead, she said, "Thanks."

"I find it interesting," the woman continued, pondering the cover, "your use of burning as metaphor."

Teresa blushed and looked into the woman's dark eyes behind tortoise shell glasses. "I didn't catch your name," she smiled.

"I didn't toss it out," the woman smiled back. "It's Day Mansfield."

"Day," Teresa repeated. "What a great name."

"My mother was a morning person," Day explained with a smirk. "I have a younger sister named Sunny."

"Tom," Teresa said later on the phone, "I met this terrific woman on the subway." She and Day had stopped at the Peacock Cafe for coffee and cannoli. Day coincidentally lived on West Twelfth Street, just blocks from Teresa.

Teresa knew Tom would be awake, even though it was after eleven-thirty. He had recently started writing his novel again and found he could only concentrate late at night.

"Yeah?" he said without intonation, seeming distracted or bothered. "So tell me. Let's hear the dish."

"Her name is Day," Teresa said simply. "Isn't that great? I mean, wouldn't you love to call one of your characters Day?"

"Very androgynous."

Teresa reviewed the brief encounter with Day for Tom and wondered aloud if she was enthralled mostly because Day had read a deeper meaning into her book.

"You've said before that you're always looking for a perfect critic," Tom noted. "Someone who'll understand your work completely." She heard the faint crack of a match and a slow intake of breath. "I've always thought you meant something else by that."

"What?" she asked quickly.

"Someone to understand *you* completely, not your work."

As bad as it was for him, she loved the sound of his smoking. It was slow, rhythmic, comforting in its sameness.

"You're too perceptive for your own good, Tom Snow," she laughed. "Sometimes I wonder if you aren't really a woman!"

. . .

THE VOICE on the phone was amazingly unfamiliar. At first Teresa thought it was a woman from work who would never be calling her at home, because their friendship was relegated to chats at the coffee maker.

"Marianne?" Teresa asked cautiously.

"No, it's Robin. Robin Eisen."

Teresa didn't know what to say so she simply repeated "Robin." Her tongue took up too much room in her mouth.

After Robin left, Teresa had waited for her to call. Every time she got home and spied the blinking light of the answering machine, she thought, "It's a message from Robin."

There was only one message after they'd collected their things from each other's apartments, and it came a month after the break-up: "I found a pair of your jeans and some socks I don't recognize. I'll send them to you." But she never even did that. Robin's expressed desire to be platonic friends dried up in the heat of her new affair. And Teresa let Jamie's illness distract her from feeling hurt. Somehow it was easy to let two years go by with no contact.

"I . . . I heard about Jamie," Robin continued, her voice trembling. Was she emotional about Jamie, or about talking to Teresa? "I was really sad to hear."

Teresa warned herself, *Don't cry, don't let her know her words can still affect you that way, don't give her that power over you.* But Jamie had only been dead a week, and Teresa cried a lot, sometimes at just the mention of his name, and every time she saw Tom. The loss felt like something heavy sitting on her heart. She sniffed into the receiver and couldn't answer.

"Teresa?"

"Tom told me," she said shakily, "that you visited Jamie in the hospital. I appreciate it."

"Sure," Robin said, "I wanted to. It was nothing."

Teresa blew her nose. "No, it's definitely something."

The pause was no more than a few seconds, and Robin

hurried to fill it in.

"I just wanted to call and say . . . well, you know this. I thought . . . I think he was one of the best," she finished a bit clumsily, but with a deepness of emotion that Teresa felt snaking through the phone line.

Teresa suddenly forgot that years had gone by silently. She blurted out, "I can't tell you how much I lost," making herself open and fragile and vulnerable. "The other night a friend of his called to offer his condolences, a guy I don't know very well, and for some reason he called me 'sweetie.' He said, 'I'm here for you, sweetie,' or something like that. That's what Jamie called me since I was little. Do you remember that? I mean, since I can remember, that's who I was with Jamie. And I was very short with this guy and practically hung up on him, but I didn't want to cry or worse yet, scream. He must have thought I was really rude. I don't know what got into me."

"I'm sure he understood on some level," Robin said kindly, "even if he didn't know what he said."

Teresa blew her nose again and wondered why she felt so warm toward Robin after so much time and all that had happened between them. She had an irresistible urge to tease her.

"Say, Robin," she said, still sniffling a little, "you never sent back my jeans. Remember? What did you do, sell them on the street for extra cash?"

Robin chuckled, a touch of embarrassment in her voice. "I can't believe you remembered! I just never got to the post office," she confessed. "Then I started working out and I lost ten pounds and they fit me. So I . . . kept them. You know," she laughed, "I think I'm wearing them now."

"Well, I have something of yours, too," Teresa disclosed. "Your Pep Boys tee-shirt. It was in my laundry bag when you left. I wear it a lot."

"Yeah, I wondered what happened to that," Robin said.

There was a gap in the conversation, and Teresa was thankful that Robin didn't say anything meaningless or untrue to spoil the moment like "I'll call again. Sorry it's been so long."

"Thanks for calling," Teresa said. "And for visiting Jamie."

"Sure," Robin said again. "Sure."

They hung up, and Teresa left her hand on the receiver for a few seconds.

．　．　．

DAY CAME up for air. She smiled at Teresa. "How're we doing?" she asked dreamily.

"Great," Teresa smiled back, tense and forced. "It feels great." She was fully aware of how long it was taking her to come, and she worried about the stamina of Day's tongue. She felt distracted and just inches from crying, but couldn't imagine letting that happen in bed with a near-stranger.

Day slid up beside Teresa and placed her lips right against her ear. "Is there something else you want?" she whispered in her throaty voice.

"No...I...I'm sorry," Teresa stumbled, the tears welling up. "I just can't seem to...it's been a while since...Do you think we should be practicing safe sex?" It seemed all wrong, having sex with Jamie dead.

"Don't apologize," Day said, smoothing Teresa's hair. "We talked about safe sex and decided we didn't need to, right?"

Day was Teresa's attempt at being casual. They had only known each other two weeks, during which Day had quickly ushered their relationship from coffee to dinner out in the neighborhood to dinner at her apartment. They'd talked over that dinner for five hours, with Day's face becoming more and more animated and her voice deeper and richer in the candlelight as the date progressed. After five hours, though,

Teresa's inclination was to go home, to retreat from Day's expectations. Still, when over the decaf Day suggested she spend the night, Teresa decided it couldn't hurt. As she'd gotten to know her, Teresa was less entranced with Day than she had been the first night they met on the subway. Insightful observations weren't always falling from her lips. But it had been over two years since Teresa had had sex with anyone, closer to three if only good sex counted. The very last time she made love with Robin, Teresa had had too much to drink and fell asleep in the middle. Later, she regretted that had been their finale. She wondered if that's how Robin would remember her and if she would mention it to her new lover.

Teresa was sure she was a disappointing date. Her hand wandered tentatively to Day's breast, but Day covered it with her own hand.

"Maybe this is just the wrong time," Day suggested. "It's late, we could go to sleep."

"You're mad," Teresa observed.

"No," Day insisted firmly.

"Disappointed."

"Well," Day conceded, "just a little. I do want you. But only if you want to be wanted."

Wanting to be wanted. Teresa pondered that a moment, tossed it from one end of her thoughts to the other. She liked being wanted, she loved being adored. "You know, I adore you," Tom routinely told her now, and it never failed to make her blush and smile shyly. But Tom's adoration was safe, close and detached at the same time. His only expectation was that she offer him the same sort of trouble-free love, which she happily did. It let her experience intimacy without any of the hassles.

She thought to tell Day, "I want to be wanted, but I'm not sure by whom," but decided against it as being too truthful. She didn't want to hurt her feelings, though she suspected this night would probably be their last date.

"It's me, not you," Teresa said sadly, already mourning the loss of potential. She had no prospects but Day, and that already felt lonely, ending it before it began. Every hour during the short night, she woke up with a start, until the sun came up and she rose to pick her clothes off the floor where she'd shed them six hours earlier.

"I'll call you," Teresa lied, and Day's saying, "That would be good," she suspected, was just as big an untruth.

. . .

"You'll be pleased to know," Tom announced on the phone, "my gland is back to normal. I told you it was the fucking weather."

"Happy Gay Day," she said, tapping her juice glass to the receiver.

. . .

"What's this?" she asked. Teresa picked Tom up after work to go to a movie. While he opened his mail, she checked out the book he was reading and found a handful of loose coins tossed next to it on the coffee table. Among them was a large, flat token, like something from an arcade or carnival. She picked it up and examined it, cradled it thoughtfully in her palm.

"*Borrowed Time*," he answered, thinking she meant the book. He was busy with a stack of bills and didn't notice that she was holding the token up for him to see. "You should read it, it's wonderful."

"No," Teresa corrected. She had already read the book and was almost certain she'd recommended it to him. It annoyed her a little that he didn't remember. "I mean this thing. This token, or whatever it is. What have you been doing, running out to Coney Island?"

Tom looked up, flushed as if he *had* just stepped off a

148

roller coaster. His face was a study in confusion. He didn't seem to know whether to smile sheepishly or chastise her for poking into his things.

"Oh, Teresa," he said, like a teenager caught by his mother.

"What?" she asked, thoroughly confused. "'Oh, Teresa' what?"

He slit open a bill distractedly. The letter opener snagged and ripped the invoice and its envelope, and Tom's smile vanished. "It's from the Triple X Video on Fourteenth Street, if you really want to know," he said finally, hurriedly, maybe hoping she'd miss it.

"Oh," she said, a soft syllable that got lost in the space between them.

"I don't make a habit of going," he continued, though she hadn't asked. "I've only been twice, actually, about two weeks ago and then this afternoon. It's no big deal. It's completely safe."

She stared down at the token, which suddenly had added weight. Quietly, she let it drop with a clink to its place among the dimes and nickels on the table. "Oh," she said again.

"You buy those," he went on—why was he going on?— "and then you go into these booths and watch porn."

"What's the attraction?" she asked, her eyes still focused on the shiny token. "You could rent porn at home."

Tom cleared his throat. "The booths are glass. There are other guys in the other ones," he explained. "You can, well, watch each other."

"Oh," she said a third time, having difficulty visualizing it, not really daring to visualize it. She didn't know why it bothered her, it seemed totally harmless, but Tom at the Triple X Video felt like an abandonment. Of Jamie, whose side of the bed hadn't been cold for long. And of her. She thought she knew Tom, but she didn't understand his desire to expose himself to strangers.

And she felt something besides annoyance, in spite of herself, something vaguely like arousal. Men had so much less inhibition around sex. Even Jamie, raised Catholic like she was, had overcome his prudish religious upbringing.

"Well, I hope it was fun," she said cavalierly, trying to clear her thoughts and sweep away the conversation. Still, she couldn't stop wondering what the other men had been like, the ones Tom had jerked off with that afternoon. Did he notice their faces, or was that not the point?

.   .   .

THE MOVIE they saw after Jamie's memorial was *Back to the Future, Part III*, though neither Tom nor Teresa's father had seen Parts I and II. They chose it because it was the only movie at the Cineplex near Tom's apartment that didn't require thinking. Teresa sat between Tom and her father. Midway through the movie, Tom groped for her hand from one direction and she grasped her father's from the other, and the three of them sat in tenuous connection through the rest of it.

Afterwards her father asked, "Why did we see that?"

Teresa burst out laughing, but when she saw his serious face, she cut herself short. Tom coughed.

"It's a family tradition," Teresa said. "Remember? When Alison was buried, Jamie took me to the movies."

Her father blinked several times very quickly. She wondered when he had last thought of Alison and what passed through his mind when he did. It had been twenty-six years, a complete lifetime in the age of AIDS.

"I remember that," he said slowly, cautiously, as if he were afraid to remember. "I gave him hell."

"Yeah, I overheard you," Teresa said. Tom looked away, as if he'd accidentally stepped into an intimate family moment and didn't know how to extricate himself. Or else he was looking away because he didn't want his own memory of Jamie in the Howard Johnson's parking lot to show so plainly on his face. "You must have been incredibly angry."

"I was," her father quickly agreed. "I thought it was a stupid thing to do, making the day into a party."

"No," she countered, "I mean, you must have been incredibly angry about Alison dying."

Tom stepped off the sidewalk away from them and crossed Broadway. Teresa watched him sprint agilely in front of a passing cab.

"Dad?"

Her father's eyes had fallen and rested on his shoes, which were highly polished to a gleaming black. He still wore wingtips, had always worn them, even when they'd fallen out of fashion. He was now once again in style. Wingtips on anyone, even women, reminded Teresa of him.

"Do you ever think about her?"

His lips parted several times and closed again.

"When it first happened, her dying," Teresa began, "I thought about her all the time. I pretended she was still alive. I don't know exactly when I stopped. But one day, I couldn't remember what she was like anymore. Not how she sounded, not what she was like when she was happy. We never *talked* about her. That's when she really died."

She took his arm, because he seemed to be rooted to the sidewalk, and guided him across Broadway.

"With Jamie," she continued, though she felt like she was rambling, "at least I got a chance to prepare. I've spent months consciously thinking about how to remember what he was *like*, memorizing it, in fact."

"Meaning?" her father, asked after a pause.

"Meaning, you know, little things like his inflection when he called me 'sweetie,' the way he used his hands when

151

he talked. Things he believed in, places he loved to go. What he was *like*."

Her father faced her at the other side of Broadway with her fingers still gripping his arm. "When Alison was a baby," he said, "she never cried. Even when she hurt herself or wanted to be fed. Oh, maybe she cried a handful of times. But your mother and I always talked about what a happy girl she'd be. She was so good we thought everyone who told us babies kept you up all night was crazy. Then," he paused with a smile, "you came along, and we knew what they meant."

Teresa smiled and lightened her touch. He shook his head and a puzzled look clouded his face. "There's a lot I've forgotten, too," he acknowledged. "A lot of things that happened between then and the hospital. Your mother," he continued sadly, "still won't let me mention her name. It's almost like she never existed."

"Maybe some day you could force her to talk about it," Teresa suggested. "Just say, 'Eileen, I'd like to talk to you about Alison's death.' Just like that. Tell her because of Jamie you're thinking about it again."

"Twenty-six years later?"

"Why not?" she asked. "My hunch is that she's blamed herself all this time. For not being God. You know, for not being able to save Alison." Teresa glanced ahead of them and spotted Tom staring into a hardware store window, his hands clasped firmly behind him. He seemed to be considering the sale price of charcoal briquets. Teresa and her father walked up behind him and their reflections met his in the glass.

"Who barbecues in Manhattan?" he wondered aloud. "I mean, where do people do it? There aren't enough back yards and terraces to warrant all the charcoal they sell."

Teresa smiled. "Let's go back to Tom's place and eat," she suggested.

The two men exchanged a glance of caution and unfamiliarity.

"Oh, come on," she said, taking both their arms. "You have to eat, don't you?"

. . .

TOM DIRECTED Teresa's father to the extension in the study for privacy, but he insisted that the living room phone was fine.

"Eileen? It's Richard." After almost forty years of marriage, Teresa thought, didn't they recognize each other's voices? She half expected him to continue, "Richard, Richard Keenan."

"It was fine . . . No, we haven't eaten yet . . . I don't know, a lot of his friends, I guess . . . No, I didn't . . . Yes, I made sure of that."

What? she wondered. Not to shake hands with any of them? Not to exchange bodily fluids? When it came to her mother, Teresa expected the worst. Her father lowered his voice slightly.

"It's fine, Eileen, really . . . No . . . No . . . Yes, eleven thirty-five tomorrow . . . What? Yes, we'll be eating soon . . . Yes, all right . . . Do you want to talk to Teresa? . . . All right, then . . . I'll tell her. Good night."

He nestled the receiver back onto the phone. "Your mother says hello. She couldn't talk, she was on her way out to the church bazaar with Mrs. DeNardo."

Her father settled in the chair across from her and Tom on the sofa. Tom was fidgeting with an assortment of take-out menus, shuffling them back and forth in his hands like a big deck of cards. Teresa hadn't wanted to talk to her mother anyway. She was afraid she would scream into the phone, *Why the fuck didn't you come?*, and she knew that would start a battle that she didn't have the energy for. She couldn't tell if that's what her anger was about anyway. It felt like something deeper, something that grew bigger inside her every day.

. . .

WEEKS AFTER the memorial, Tom was still holding onto Jamie's ashes. Teresa was not sure where he kept the canister, but she knew it was somewhere in the apartment. She asked about it several times but stopped when she never got much of an answer.

On a Saturday afternoon they were sitting at the boat basin in Central Park watching children launch their toy boats off the edge. Next to them a little boy was pouting to his father because his expensive F.A.O. Schwartz sailboat had been sideswiped and sent off course by the smaller, more efficient homemade boat of two sisters. The elder of the two girls high-fived her sister.

"They remind me of my sister and me," Teresa said thoughtfully. "She was always initiating some kind of adventure, and I tagged along. Sometimes I wonder if she would have been a lesbian, too. That would have sent my mother over the edge!"

Tom caught the eye of the older sister and gave her a thumbs-up.

"Hey," Teresa said, "guess what? I finished one of the last scenes in my book. I only have about twenty pages left, I think."

"That's great," Tom said proudly, his focus shifting back to her. "Mazel tov."

"I actually sort of based the scene on a conversation we had not too long ago," she continued cautiously.

"You and me?" he asked, perplexed.

"Yeah. About Jamie's ashes. Remember? Well, in my book, they can't decide what to do with Mark's either. That seemed so real to me, so much closer to life. Things aren't always as neat and romantic as we'd like or as writers make them."

"No," he agreed quietly, "they certainly aren't."

"But do you think too many novels are using that same idea? The indecision around the ashes? I could change it."

"No," Tom said again, "it's a recurring question."

For a few minutes there was only the sound of children's squeals of laughter.

"So," Tom said. "You want to talk about the ashes, I guess?"

"The only place I keep coming up with is Route 17," Teresa said with a little smile. "It was the last time he was well, that trip we made to Pal's. But that's so silly. I mean, it's irreverent, don't you think? It has no real meaning, and it's so banal Jamie would *kill* us."

Tom laughed, "You won't believe this, but I came up with Route 17, too, and rejected it. We just *couldn't*."

"Maybe we're just trying too hard for meaning. Maybe we just won't ever come up with any," Teresa added.

"Well," Tom said softly, "I can't keep the canister in my desk forever. I know it's just some sort of perverse comfort. The ashes aren't *him*, for God's sake. I know I have to do something with them."

She turned back to the sisters, but they had taken their victorious boat and gone.

* * *

TERESA HAD ruined two Christmases in a row for herself by spending them with her parents. The first year, she decided on Pittsburgh for the holidays because she couldn't face New York without Robin. But she spent Christmas moping and wishing she were back in New York. The second year, when Jamie cornered her while they were shopping at Macy's and tried to convince her to stay in the city with him and Tom, she couldn't think of any good reason not to, except something that sounded suspiciously like guilt.

"Mom told me they weren't planning on having Christmas," Teresa explained. Standing on prolonged register lines with him, watching him buy cotton sweaters, silk ties, leather gloves, an espresso maker, she lost mental count of the small fortune Jamie was spending on Tom alone.

"What does that mean?" Jamie asked sharply, handing her two packages to carry.

"That means no tree, no presents, no nothing," Teresa elaborated. "She said there was nothing to celebrate, they're just getting old and there are no grandchildren." Jamie sighed.

Outside people jammed the sidewalk, trying to view Macy's window decorations. Jamie nudged her onto the line that was teeming with parents and squirming children.

"So what should I do with Mom? Say fuck you, be that way, *I'm* going to have a Merry Christmas without you in New York?" Teresa asked.

"No," Jamie said, "you're too nice for that. And if you stayed here, you'd let your Catholic guilt ruin your holiday anyway."

The windows accommodated a three-story Victorian dollhouse with elaborate gingerbread, complete with a perfect family in period costumes—Mother in the parlor in green velvet, Father in the library in a brocade smoking jacket, Sister at her vanity in a silk wrapper, Brother in his bedroom in a navy blue sailor suit. Outside, in the powdery snow, joyful guests approached for Christmas dinner. "Look at that little fur muff she's wearing!" the woman next to Teresa pointed out to her small daughter. "And see the sleigh? That's how people used to get around without cars."

Music blared from the P.A. system, a sweetly repetitious "Winter Wonderland" that, after five or ten minutes on line, began to wear thin with Teresa.

"These windows are so much less interesting than they

used to be," Jamie observed, "even ten years ago. The figures don't even move! When I was a kid in Pittsburgh, the big family outing used to be to go to see Kaufmann's Christmas windows on a Saturday afternoon. They were different every year. Macy's windows always look the same to me now. No imagination anymore." The woman turned to him disapprovingly, as if to warn him not to spoil the experience for her child, and Jamie pulled Teresa off the line.

"So what's to be done about Eileen?" he asked. "How did you leave it with her?"

"I told her I was going to come and buy the goddamn tree and trim it and bring them presents whether they liked it or not," Teresa said. "I call it Christmas-by-Force."

Jamie looked skeptical. "Your mother's a strong woman," he warned. "You won't get her to do anything she doesn't want to, especially have a good time."

"It's just three days," Teresa noted. "What's three days?"

Her parents met her at the airport on Christmas Eve. She only saw them once a year, and each time she was startled by how they'd aged. Did they look at her with the same surprise, she wondered—did they see in her their own mortality?

"What kind of haircut is that?" her mother asked, laughing nervously, after she pecked her on the cheek.

"Well, merry Christmas," Teresa replied icily, realizing that sometimes three days could seem like months. "It's a short one, Mother."

"It's too short if you ask me," her mother concluded.

Teresa's first impulse was to snap, "Well, no one did." They were, after all, not really talking about haircuts, but about Teresa being a lesbian. Teresa chose a calmer, joking approach instead. "Well, you're the one who started me out with short cuts, Mom, remember? That awful pixie cut when I was ten?"

157

"Oh," her mother smiled, the chill thawing, "that *was* bad. Poor Trix wasn't very good at anything but cutting off split ends!"

"Whatever happened to that shop?"

"She closed it and moved to Miami Beach," her mother said. "Made enough money from bad haircuts to buy a condo!"

"Actually," her father chimed in, "it was the cash from selling the shop that bought the condo. Some developer bought the whole block and sold it to Burger King." It was the first thing he'd said beyond "Hi, honey."

Her parents' street was dark except for some red, white and green lights along the railing and overhang of what had been the Schultz's house when Teresa was growing up. Now it belonged to the Tulicettis.

"Looks like the Italian flag," her mother remarked.

An artificial tree commanded the living room window of her parents' house. It was already decorated with an assortment of silver balls and strings of colored lights. Teresa stared at it in confusion, not just because her mother had threatened not to have a tree, but because her parents had always been Christmas tree snobs. Only the freshest, fullest Scotch pines for them, bought just days before Christmas and trimmed on Christmas Eve.

"You got a fake tree," Teresa said critically, thinking as she said it, *I sound like her.*

"Oh, I can't stand the mess anymore," her mother explained. "And your father can't be bothered. You get older, you lose the spirit. This one I can do myself. $79.95 at Sears, and we'll have it for the rest of our lives."

Teresa's father had sold major appliances at Gimbel's department store for years, all the time she lived at home. When Gimbel's went out of business in the mid-eighties, he went to work at Sears at the South Hills Village Mall selling small appliances, toasters and Cuisinarts. It was a step down they didn't talk about. He was sixty-three and hoping to retire in a few years anyway, but he had no pension from his job and had had to put money aside in CD's and IRA's for the years to come.

"Without me, he'd just spend his money," her mother laughed nervously. "I've had to scrimp and save so we wouldn't be homeless in our old age."

"Oh, Mom," Teresa said, not really meaning it but unable to stop herself anyway, "you'll always have a home with me."

"Yeah, I can see us all in that closet in New York," her mother laughed again.

They ate ham and cheese sandwiches and Campbell's tomato soup, because her mother didn't want to cook and wouldn't let Teresa. "You're on vacation!" she said. Her parents ate quickly and without feeling, but Teresa purposefully lingered over her food, chewing each bite much longer than necessary. All the while she was wondering if Tom had prepared the salmon recipe he'd recently found and if he and Jamie were having dinner alone or with friends.

"With friends," Jamie said at midnight when she called. "Leo and Ken, whom you know. And Steven Clark, whom you don't."

"Who are Steve and Clark?"

"No," he laughed, "it's just one person—Steven Clark."

"Why did you do that?" her mother asked when she got off the phone ten minutes later. "You see them all the time, don't you?"

"I wanted to say Merry Christmas," she snapped. "Is that so horrible? He may not make it to another."

After that she wasn't in the mood to exchange presents, but they did anyway. Teresa hurriedly downed some eggnog laced with bourbon and fixed herself another.

"You can always just stay drunk," Jamie had suggested on the phone when she responded evasively to the question,

"How's everything there?"

Teresa's parents gave her a woolen scarf and a check for thirty dollars, which she accepted matter-of-factly. For ten years they'd been giving her scarves, socks or slippers with a check for thirty dollars. It was unclear how they'd arrived at that figure. Once it had bought a toaster oven, a pair of pants, a number of cassettes. Now with inflation it covered cab fare from the airport to her house with enough left over for some take-out Chinese food.

She bought them a garage door opener.

"You think we can't open our own door anymore?" her mother said. "Are you telling us we're old?"

"No," Teresa replied, her foot tapping the carpet nervously, "that never even occurred to me."

"It's nice, honey," her father said.

"You know, we could get this at Sears with our discount," her mother pointed out. "Do you want to take it back and we'll get a cheaper one here?"

"No," Teresa said again, getting up for a refill of eggnog, "I don't."

When her senses and feelings were dulled with bourbon, Teresa slumped in her chair and watched the blinking tree lights. In her childhood, the individual lights used to flicker at different intervals, now they flashed on and off in unison like a neon sign. She mentioned this.

Her mother thought a moment, staring at the tree. "No," she finally disagreed, "they never flickered."

Teresa didn't argue, because it could have been her imagination. A vague, hazy memory of trying to count the tree lights with Alison stirred in her mind.

"Alison and I used to try to count the lights," she said, "but we always lost our place and never finished."

"There have always been forty-eight," her mother replied. "Two strings of twenty-four each." She ignored the reference to Alison.

"It was more fun to try to count them ourselves," Teresa smiled. "We'd just start laughing hysterically."

Her mother stood up abruptly and left the room. Her father twirled the ice cubes in his drink. Rather than sit in silence with him, Teresa followed her mother to the kitchen, where she was standing at the sink, looking down at the dirty dishes stacked there. Her back heaved with a big sigh, then she turned and jumped at seeing Teresa.

"Oh," she said with a startled bounce.

"You okay?" Teresa asked. "What's going on?"

"I thought I'd bring in some chips and dip," her mother said quietly. "Would you like some chips and dip?"

"I'm not hungry," Teresa said. "I'm fine." *But are you?* she wanted to ask.

Instead there was an impossible silence, her mother apparently unable to think of another reason to be in the kitchen, Teresa wanting to push her into talking but not sure how. She'd never learned to challenge her mother, and so she almost never did. The few times she tried, the words came out all wrong, bitter and accusatory and ultimately not at all helpful.

"I think I'll just do these dishes then," her mother said, turning back to the sink and running the tap. She said something else, but Teresa couldn't hear it over the water.

"Mom?" she said, loud enough to be heard in the next room. Her mother jumped again.

"I thought you'd gone," her mother said, and when she turned her head slightly, Teresa saw she had started to cry. Suddenly her mother covered her face with soapy hands. "Why do you do these things? Are you trying to upset me?" Her voice was muffled and weak.

"What things?" Teresa probed, knowing very well. "What things do I do?"

"We were having a nice time until you brought up . . ."

"Alison," Teresa finished.

"You know it hurts me to talk about it," her mother sniffled, lowering her hands and blotting her face with a paper towel.

"All I did was mention her name," Teresa pointed out. "Something's wrong if after twenty years I can't even mention her name. You never let me talk about her! Not once! It's the great Alison Keenan cover up. There," she added bitterly, "I said her name again."

Teresa's mother said something into the sink that sounded like "It wasn't my fault." Teresa wanted to say she knew that, that no one blamed her, but she was sure her mother would never believe it. Parents must always think they can save their children, even when they have no control. Teresa put a hand on her shoulder, thinking about the burden her mother had carried around all those years since Alison died.

"Let's go back into the living room," Teresa coaxed. "It's Christmas Eve, and you don't have to do the dishes. Dad's in there all by himself."

Her mother dried her eyes with the paper towel again and blew her nose. Her eyes were red, and Teresa's father would notice but not comment on it. Teresa wondered when he had given up commenting on it.

"What were you two doing in there?" he asked jovially. He had put on an Andy Williams tape, and "The Christmas Song" was playing.

"The dishes," Teresa replied, finally letting go of her mother's shoulder.

．　．　．

"WHAT DO you think we'll look like when we're old?" Alison asked, as the two of them stood in front of the mirror in their room. The top of Teresa's head reached Alison's nose, but aside from their height difference, they looked remarkably the same. Alison's body was thinner, leaner, but their faces were almost identical, round and pink with deep-set green eyes. "I mean, when we're thirty."

For Teresa it was hard to imagine thirty, so she didn't answer. She was eight. Sometimes it felt like she'd always been eight, that she always would be. Their mother was thirty-three, their father thirty-seven. She had seen photographs of them as children but could not connect the childish faces with her adult parents.

Alison was pinning up her long wavy hair with some bobby pins furtively removed from the bathroom. "I'll be thirty in 1982," she said, having difficulty getting the pins to stay put. Her hair was fine and silky, like Teresa's; even barrettes slipped through it. "You'll be thirty in 1984." Alison was learning about years in school, but they were still an enigma to Teresa. She knew it was 1962 only because Alison had told her. "I'll always be older than you."

"Maybe someday," Teresa said, "you'll stop getting older and I'll pass you up!" She pushed a few pins randomly into her own hair as she watched Alison fuss with some re-calcitrant wisps.

"*Im*-possible," Alison declared. "When elephants fly." To test her new hairstyle, she gave her head a little shake, and the pins fell with small tinkles to the floor. Undaunted, Alison began replacing them in her hair one by one.

Teresa removed the pins from her own hair and concentrated on watching and advising Alison. "There's a piece you missed," she said, touching it lightly, always surprised at the feel of Alison's hair, so much like her own.

"I'll be an actress and live in Hollywood, right near the ocean," Alison continued. "Let's think up a name for me. Actresses always change their names."

Teresa thought a moment and asked, "Why?"

"Oh, everyone does it. You will, too, when you get married," Alison noted. "Mommy's name wasn't always Keenan."

"What was it?" Teresa asked, bewildered.

"Scanlon," Alison said, stuffing three pins into the same unruly strand. "Eileen Frances Scanlon. Isn't that pretty? Then she married Daddy and it changed. What should I change mine to? I kind of like the name Alison. Let's just think of a new last name."

Teresa could only think of the names of people she knew—Schmidt, Costello, Masetti.

"No, no, *no*," Alison said, frowning. "Something like a movie star. Alison Day. Alison Monroe. What do you think?"

"Alison Day," Teresa repeated. "That's pretty."

"Maybe I'll have to change the Alison, too," she decided, squinting at her reflection. Her hair was finally up, with dozens of black bobby pins peeking through the honey-colored waves. "Maybe I'll be Pamela Day."

Teresa couldn't imagine Alison with the name Pamela. Changing the Keenan part was okay, but a new first name would be hard to adjust to. Could she still call her Alison? Would she still be her sister? Who would Pamela Day be?

"Don't change your first name, please," Teresa pleaded into the mirror. "I don't like the name Pamela."

"How about Michele?" Alison pinched her own cheeks the way she'd seen their mother do it. She stood away from the mirror to view her creation. "Ladies and gentlemen— Miss Michele Monroe!"

Teresa stared at her own reflection. Her eyes were misting over. "If you change your name," she pouted, "I'll never speak to you again."

"Promise?" Alison asked, turning suddenly snotty, the way she did sometimes. Or maybe it was Miss Michele Monroe being mean. Teresa left the mirror and went to sit on her bed with Dr. Seuss's *The 500 Hats of Bartholomew Cubbins*, which she had just checked out of the library. She refused to look at her sister until she had taken down her hair and become Alison again.

. . .

THERE WAS more room at Tom's, but Teresa's father opted to stay with her at her crowded apartment. "I don't know Tom very well," he said, visibly nervous. "It would be awkward. He'd probably like to be alone after the memorial."

"Actually, he'd probably like company," Teresa replied. "But maybe it would be a little weird."

She offered her father the bedroom, but he insisted on taking the pull-out sofa. It was old and the cover was worn, but the innerspring mattress inside was still comfortable. Her father bounced on it a few times while she rummaged through her closet looking for coordinating sheets. All she came up with were bedclothes of various mismatched shades of blue.

"Sorry, Dad, it's not the Hilton," she laughed as they made the bed together. "I guess I could use a new set of sheets for company."

"I'll make a note of that for Christmas," he said eagerly, proud of his idea. "They have some nice sheets at Sears. That's where your mother buys ours now."

It was a sticky night, the air heated and thick, and her father said no to the light blanket she proposed. "Do these windows open any wider?" he asked, struggling with one that was jammed midway in the frame.

"That's about it," she said. "Sorry, it's . . ."

" . . . not the Hilton," he finished with a smile.

After he got a glass of water, it looked as if he planned to retire with the evening paper. She was finishing *Borrowed Time*, and was eager to get back to it. Since she'd started it a few days earlier, she had been almost unable to put it down. Paul Monette's privileged life was so unlike her own, but his accurate rendering of the face of AIDS stirred her memories of Jamie.

"So what time do you want to get up tomorrow, Dad?" she asked to close the evening. "Your plane's at eleven-thirty, right?"

"Oh, I wake up automatically at around seven," he said. "Internal alarm. I should probably leave here around nine-thirty, I guess."

"That sounds about right," she replied. "Well, I think I'll turn in now. Unless there's anything else you need. You've got a towel and washcloth."

"Yes, here they are." He fingered them lightly and looked at her as if he had one more thing to say.

"So, good night then, I guess," she said.

"Good night, honey." She was in her room with the door halfway closed when he called to her. "Teresa?"

"Yes, Dad?" She held her hand on the knob, prepared to be either detained or dismissed. "Do you need anything?"

"I just wanted to say something," he answered slowly. He was standing next to the pull-out bed looking confused and anxious, as if he had in fact chosen to stay in the home of a perfect stranger. "Actually, to tell you something."

Teresa returned to the living room and faced him at the opposite end of the bed. In the dim light of the living room, his light hair brushed back neatly from his forehead, he looked for a single moment like an older Jamie.

"What is it?" she asked, averting her eyes.

"It's just that there are things your mother never talks about that would be helpful for you to know, I think," he offered. "Things I forget sometimes myself. It came to me earlier, when you were talking about Alison, that you might want to know."

"Know what?" she inquired, suddenly conscious of her heart beating hard in her chest, like it wanted to get out.

"Years ago, your mother had a miscarriage," he said.

"Before Alison, when we were first married."

Teresa's mouth fell open in surprise. "A miscarriage," she repeated, unsure why it would have been kept from her, when there was no stigma attached to miscarriage that she was aware of. "Why didn't she say anything?"

"It was devastating," he replied. "I think she really believed she was to blame somehow. When she was pregnant with Alison, she stayed in bed at her parents' house for the last three months, because she lost the other in the last trimester. It was a boy. We even had a name picked out."

"What was it?" Teresa asked, wondering briefly what it would have been like to have an older brother.

"Richard John," he answered, with a deep breath that suggested he missed the possibility of a son. "The John was for my father and hers." He paused and stared at his hands. "When your mother got pregnant again," he continued, "she said a rosary every night for the baby."

Teresa knew her mother's rosary beads, the pearly pink glass ones she'd gotten from her own mother at her First Communion. When Alison was sick, Teresa could feel them bulging out of the pocket of her mother's housedress whenever she snuggled close. In the mornings, they were always laying on the night table in her parents' bedroom. Once Teresa had put them over her head like a necklace and her mother saw her and said that was sacrilegious. Later, they never lay out where Teresa could find them.

"I thought you'd like to know," her father repeated. "Maybe you won't be so . . . hard on your mother."

Teresa didn't know what to say so she said nothing. She crossed her arms and waited for her father to continue, but he had apparently finished his revelation.

"She's had a hard time," he said. "It was hard on both of us, but your mother took it worse. I had other things, you know—work, mostly."

Teresa remembered her parents' black-and-white wedding picture from 1949. At the church, they looked so young and hopeful, about to embark on the happy life her mother had imagined for herself but wouldn't know. A successful husband, children who would follow her example, grow up, marry, and have children of their own. How ill-prepared her mother had been for the changes the world would experience, how caught between two worlds. And how strange Teresa must look to her, born in a generation of daughters who had more options than women had ever known before. What was there for women like her mother, who had based their lives on a dream?

"Thanks, Dad," Teresa said simply. "It *is* good to know."

"You won't say I told?" he asked, like a kid afraid of his mother.

"No, of course not."

He was still standing when she kissed him good night, and when she went back into her bedroom, she left the door open between them.

. . .

HER PARENTS didn't ask where she was going, and she didn't tell them. She borrowed her father's car, while he nervously asked, "You sure you'll be okay? You almost never drive in New York."

"Oh, I drive Jamie's car all the time," she lied. "I'll be fine."

At a gas station on the North Side, she asked for directions to the cemetery. The attendant looked perplexed; how many people visit cemeteries in the snow the day after Christmas? The nursery at the bottom of the hill leading to the cemetery was boarded up for winter with a sign that said "See You March 15" across the door.

The road was icy, and she was concerned about getting stuck and having to walk down to the main road and signal someone. She only vaguely remembered the direction to go, but there at the crest of the hill she saw her grandparents' marker. It was dusted with white, and snow had filled in the first few letters of the name "Scanlon." Dead geranium stems twined together in front of the stone.

Next to their marker was Alison's. Teresa stared at it from the car. She'd never seen it before. Her parents had never taken her to the cemetery after Alison died, and when she grew up, she'd never traveled across town by herself to see it. Now she spotted the name in clear block letters:

MARY ALISON KEENAN
June 14, 1952–February 6, 1964

There was something in smaller print that she couldn't see from the car. Teresa put on her scarf and gloves and stepped out onto the cold, crunchy ground.

"'Suffer the little children to come unto me,'" she read aloud from the marker.

She brushed some snow from the top of the stone and without thinking, without caring how it looked or if she was showing disrespect, she sat on it.

. . .

THE SUMMER after Alison died, the Keenans' vacation routine changed forever. They had, for the last six years except one when Alison was sick, rented a cabin at Lake Erie. Teresa's father liked to fish, and her mother favored the clear air of the lake. After Alison passed away, her parents reconsidered all their choices.

"It *would* be nice to get away," Teresa overheard her mother say to her father, "but I wouldn't go back to the lake." Her mother sniffled and blew her nose.

"No, no, of course not," her father agreed. "We have to do something different." A long pause. "You know, Frank D'Alessio took his family to Gettysburg last summer for the centennial. It was educational and not too far away. You know it would be different from what we've done before. More sightseeing, less relaxing..."

"Oh, it's about time we did some sightseeing," her mother broke in. "It'll be good for Teresa. She starts history in the fall."

Her father began to collect maps and brochures in a shoebox with a magic marker notation on the lid: *Gettysburg Trip.* He got a fat package in the mail from the Gettysburg Chamber of Commerce.

"This motel looks nice and clean," he announced one night. He dipped into the shoebox after dinner instead of ice cream or cookies. "They say right here, 'Perfect for Families.'"

Her mother winked at Teresa as she scraped all the leftovers together onto one dish to throw away. "That's us," she said with a tight smile.

Her father passed her a brochure with a picture of the motel on the front. It was gray brick with white columns and a blue swimming pool. The name appeared at the top of the brochure in elaborate script: *Blue and Gray Motor Lodge.* Teresa flipped the brochure open to a picture of what was indeed a "nice and clean" room. It had two double beds with flowered bedspreads and a desk and TV by the window. In the picture a family—a mother, father, boy and girl—were in the middle of a happy moment. The children were smiling while the mother read to them from a brochure and the father lit his pipe.

On the back of the brochure a map showed other local attractions. "We'll try to see all of them," her father said eagerly. "Maybe go through Pennsylvania Dutch country."

It was their first car trip without Alison, the first one where they didn't have to carry a container for the times Alison got car sick. The plastic container was still in the trunk when Teresa's father began packing the car for the trip. He removed it without a word and set it reverently on the floor of the garage.

Uncle Jamie was there, collecting the keys to the house so he could check it while they were gone. He chuckled over the plastic container. "Alison's puke jar!" he laughed. "God, she couldn't go five minutes in a car without throwing up. I still have a container for her in my trunk, too." He was suddenly wistful.

Teresa's father ignored the reminiscing and carefully checked his spare. He traced its contours with his fingertips, bounced it on the floor of the garage a few times and inserted a pressure gauge. "You know, Jamie," he said after a pause, releasing the gauge with a satisfied pop, "I don't mind talking about Alison, but it wouldn't be good for you to say what you just said in front of Eileen." He glanced in Teresa's direction, but she pretended not to pay attention so they would keep talking.

"If you ask me," Jamie countered, "Eileen would do better to talk about Alison once in a while. She keeps it all bottled up."

"She's doing fine."

Teresa kept her eyes in her lap, where she was putting together and taking apart a chain of paper clips. She was imagining the clips had a bunch of keys at the end that opened a lot of secret doors. Doors like the one at school where the teachers disappeared to get supplies. Doors like at St. Sebastian's convent, where the nuns lived in tiny cells. Doors like the one leading to Grandma's basement, where Teresa wasn't allowed to go. "Too cold," Grandma explained, "and damp."

Her father packed the family suitcases on one side of the spare tire. From the look of things, they'd be gone for a while, but she thought her father had told Jamie "a long weekend."

"Sometimes," Jamie persisted, "it's good to get some

171

counseling. For the whole family. My friend Tom might know . . . "

"That's not necessary," her father answered, slamming the trunk closed. "We're all doing fine now, aren't we?" He chucked Teresa's chin in a way that was unfamiliar to her. She returned to her paper clips. The only sound in the garage was the tiny click of metal clips against each other as she hooked and released them, hooked and released them.

"Well," Jamie said finally, "anyway."

"We'll be back Sunday night," her father said. "Late. No need to check things more than once."

"I'll come Saturday," Jamie said, nodding. "Probably early in the afternoon."

"Big date Saturday night?" her father grinned.

"Hm, maybe," Jamie said, blushing slightly. "Well, I'll have to be heading off. You have a great time, sweetie, and have a piece of shoo-fly pie for me."

"What's shoo-fly pie?" she laughed as he bent down to kiss her hair.

"I dunno. I just like the sound of it, don't you?"

Her mother took a long time packing a lunch for the car. Much later than her father wanted, they drove out of Pittsburgh to their vacation, past choking steel mills and up and down the winding roads of western Pennsylvania.

"We're taking the scenic route," her father announced, "instead of the turnpike. This way, we'll go through the Allegheny Mountains. Sometimes the roads twist like hairpins."

But by the time they'd climbed the first curve, Teresa was lying flat on the back seat, her stomach gurgling and backfiring, her morning cereal caught in a lump in her throat. She had never been carsick once in her life, but that day outside of Somerset, her father had to pull over.

"I can't believe it," he shook his head. "I just took the container out today."

172

Her mother stroked her hair as she heaved her breakfast into a clump of weeds. Once, twice, until only dry heaves followed and her insides burned. Her mother dipped a handkerchief into cool water from a jar they carried for drinking and pressed it all over Teresa's face, then against her lips.

"Okay?" she asked.

Teresa nodded weakly. She felt chilled. She missed the rest of the mountains completely, because she was curled up on the back seat, tucked under an afghan her grandmother had crocheted.

"Can you sit up, Teresa? We're coming to Horseshoe Curve, and it's really breathtaking," her mother said.

Teresa propped herself up and glanced woozily out the window. They were in the middle of a gigantic curve, cut right around the mountains in a dizzying way. The sight of it set her head spinning, and she collapsed back onto the seat, wishing for sleep.

"So much for the scenic route," was the last thing she heard her mother say.

. . .

WHAT TERESA liked best about the Civil War battlefields was their silence and expanse. They stretched out before her and her parents as they mounted the observation tower into the sky. In the dewy late July morning the sun bounced off the cannon that had littered the fields for one hundred years.

"See all those low stone walls?" her father pointed out. "They were all there back then, too."

The thought of it made her mind race. Once, years before even her grandmother was born, soldiers built walls, fought, fell on the fields, abandoned their cannon. Fifty-one thousand died in three days, her father read from his guidebook.

"Some soldiers, especially from the South, were not much older than you," her father observed. "Thirteen, fourteen, some of them. Buglers and flag boys, mostly. Many of them never made it back."

At that Teresa's mother turned and began the descent from the tower. "Let's go," she called. "We have a lot to see."

Teresa's father filmed her climbing onto a cannon. She wasn't sure at first that she was allowed to, but there were no guards to stop people from doing it, like in the museum back home.

"Cannon are sturdy," her father said. "They've been out here in the open for a hundred years, after all." The movie camera whirred. "Eileen, you get into this, too." Later, when the movies were developed, Teresa and her mother were both looking wistfully out of the frame, off to the side.

"How about you, Daddy?"

He showed Teresa how to aim and which button to press, then took her place beside her mother, who leaned wearily on the cannon.

"That's enough of the cannon," her mother chided. "You'll have a whole movie of one silly gun."

"Where are we now?" Teresa asked, scaling rocks and scrambling up ridges. "What happened here?"

"This seems to be Devil's Den," her father said, his guidebook open to a map of thirty-five miles of battlefields.

"Now you're climbing Little Round Top." They all looked vaguely alike, miles of neat stone walls with plots of green grass tucked between them, like giant jigsaw puzzle pieces. Every so often a ridge or a glistening cannon broke the terrain.

But it was the National Cemetery that Teresa would remember most clearly and for the longest time. It unfolded before them like a city of white houses, row upon row, all exactly the same. Stone after identical stone, engraved with the name of a fallen soldier. Teresa had been to a cemetery before, to visit her grandparents' grave on Mothers' Day. It had been a family outing, a long car trip ending in a stop at a nursery at the base of the cemetery hill, where her mother purchased bright red geraniums for her parents' grave. Then the drive through the narrow, winding cemetery lanes, past plain stones, elaborate stones, mausoleums with family names carved on the front, to her grandparents' grave at the top of a ridge. One smooth stone for two—they'd died together in a car crash—a pink granite marker distinctive from the gray ones surrounding it. Teresa was careful not to step on any graves but to walk politely between the stones as her mother and father busily dug up the remains of last year's flowers and planted and watered the new ones. There was no talking, just the chirping of birds and the occasional whir of a car engine.

Teresa and Alison got bored and wandered down the ridge into a section of the cemetery across the road from their grandparents' grave, a little valley of tombstones with angels carved on them. Most of the graves were barren of flowers. She and Alison weaved in and out, Alison reading the inscriptions aloud to Teresa.

"Susan Mikulski, August 5, 1960—September 1, 1961. She was only one! Look, this one was a baby, too. And here's a boy who was four. Gosh, these are all little kids," Alison said with wonder. "I wonder why they died."

Their mother's sharp call cut through the stillness. "Alison! Teresa! Come back here! Now!"

The geraniums rooted, Teresa's mother bowed her head in a silent prayer, and Alison, Teresa and their father followed suit. But Teresa's thoughts were on the angel graves.

Now, faced with countless rows of clean, white Civil War stones, Teresa felt a rush of nausea, like she had in the car. The warm bile rose in her throat, but she swallowed it back, shuddering at the bitter taste. Her mother said nothing and stood as stiff as a tombstone in the sun. Her father raised his movie camera but lowered it without shooting.

"Union forces under General George Meade suffered 23,000 casualties," he read to them, "while Confederate troops under General Robert E. Lee sustained 28,000. It was this welter of kindred blood that moved Lincoln to compose the Gettysburg Address, appealing for peace between North and South."

Then her father began to walk down the cemetery path, looking left and right at the stones. Suddenly, he made a sharp turn into the middle of a row and walked out into the center of the cemetery. He stood there with his camera in one hand, his guidebook in the other, his back to Teresa and her mother.

Confused, Teresa glanced at her mother for reassurance. But her mother had already turned away and was wandering toward the cemetery gate. Teresa sat down on the grass next to a stone marked "Pvt. William Bennett, November 10, 1844—July 2, 1863" and waited for her father to come back to her.

* * *

GRANDMA WAS seated at the window, staring vaguely out to the curving driveway in front of the building. She had not heard them come in, though they were talking as they entered.

"Agnes," Teresa's mother said gently. She placed a hand on her shoulder and squeezed. "Agnes, it's Eileen and Richard. And look who's home for Christmas!"

Teresa hadn't seen her grandmother in her new setting. It looked vaguely like a hospital room, with two crisply made twin beds, an uncomfortable looking armchair and a framed print of Van Gogh's "Sunflowers" on the wall. For Christmas there was a small poinsettia plant on the blond dresser next to a photo of Jack Keenan, with cards taped unevenly around the mirror.

They had come with the intention of bringing her home

for Christmas Day, but the resident manager of Holy Savior Nursing Home thought it unwise. "She has moments of panic," the nun warned. "Everything becomes unfamiliar."

The last time Teresa saw her, Grandma hadn't recognized her at first but warmed up to her after about twenty minutes. "How's the Big Apple?" Grandma had asked, surprisingly remembering not only where Teresa lived but its nickname.

"She's lost almost all her vocabulary in the last few months," Teresa's mother prepared her in the car ride to the home. "There's not too much she can say anymore. Is there, Richard?" Teresa's father stared straight ahead and mumbled some reply.

"Grandma," Teresa said, bending to her cheek, "it's Teresa."

Grandma looked at her blankly and then out the window. "It snowed," she said, after some thought.

"Yes, it snowed," Teresa agreed, thinking it hopeful that Grandma could say that much.

"It's a white Christmas," Teresa's mother added perkily. "Would you like to come to our house for Christmas dinner, Agnes? To your son Richard's house? Teresa's here, it'll be like old times. Your roommate Clara went to her children for the holidays." To Teresa's father she snapped, "Say something, Richard. Don't just stand there."

"Mom," he began obediently, but then stopped and went out into the hallway.

Grandma's lips quivered, and she raised a tentative hand to pat her hair into place. "It snowed," she repeated, more emphatically. What was she thinking, Teresa wondered. Her grandmother's face was lined with confusion, like she knew the point she was trying to make but couldn't find the words in her memory. Teresa sat on the window ledge just next to her and clasped her white hand. She raised it slowly to her lips and kissed it lightly. Grandma smiled.

177

"She's a lot worse, Teresa," her mother said from the other side of the room. "I hate for you to see her like this. And your father can't take it. Maybe we should go."

"No!" Teresa said, much more loudly than she'd intended. Then more softly, "Let's stay a while. I hardly ever see her, and it's Christmas."

Her mother sat docilely in the armchair while Teresa talked to her grandmother. She told her about her job, her writing; she made one-sided small talk about the weather, thinking the idea of "snow" might spark Grandma's vocabulary. She brought her a cup of tea and some cookies from the kitchen and watched her drink the sweet, tepid liquid. "I like tea," Grandma said with a satisfied smile that made Teresa's eyes get misty.

"All these cards," Teresa's mother noted, standing at the mirror and fingering them one by one, flipping them open to read the messages. Having Alzheimer's also stripped Grandma of her privacy, Teresa thought angrily. "So many people love you, Agnes! Look, here's one from Mrs. Korbut, your old neighbor. She must be in her nineties now."

"Oh, I remember her," Teresa laughed. "I was convinced she was a witch. She had that big old wart on her nose."

"It wasn't a wart, it was a mole," her mother corrected, smiling.

"Whatever it was, it was butt ugly," Teresa said. "It had a long black hair coming out of it."

"Teresa Frances Keenan," her mother said, sitting down again, "watch your language. You have such an imagination!"

"It did, right, Grandma? Didn't Mrs. Korbut's mole have a black hair?" Teresa insisted, hoping to strike something familiar or amusing with her grandmother, so lost to her now. But Grandma was lifting the teacup again, letting the last drops slip onto her tongue. "That was good tea," was all she said.

"Would you like more, Grandma?" Teresa asked, but the question stumped her grandmother, who was busy examining the sugar cookies on the plate. She picked up each one as if considering its shape, turned it over, and replaced it carefully.

"We'd better go now, Teresa," her mother said finally. "We should find your father. He's probably out sitting in the cold car."

Teresa kissed her grandmother's cheek, which was surprisingly smooth and silky. She whispered, "I miss you" into the wisps of white hair that brushed across Grandma's ear. "Merry Christmas."

"Bye bye," Grandma answered, holding up a Santa cookie and waving it at them.

. . .

TOM HAD a set of keys made for her, because she was at the apartment twice a day. At first, remembering how she'd found them at the beach house, she hesitated to enter without ringing the bell. But Jamie was so weak from repeated infections, she realized her caution was unwarranted. She wondered when they had last had sex and what it felt like for them to know they might never have it again.

The sound of Tom's raised voice startled her as she opened the apartment door. She always thought him close to a saint for remaining even-tempered and patient with Jamie. It never occurred to her that he might lose his calm sometimes, but it made perfect sense that he did it when she wasn't around. "Well, that's what I *made* for dinner, Jamie, it's all there is. So don't eat it then—I just don't fucking care!"

Teresa clicked the door behind her. She plopped her

satchel noisily in the foyer and coughed. Then she heard the low tones of Tom's voice followed by padding footsteps.

"Teresa, hi," Tom greeted her, the stubble of his beard grazing her cheek. "You just get here?"

"Just this minute," she said nervously, wishing she had retreated when she heard the argument. "Is this a bad time?"

He pulled out his cigarettes and lit one. The hand that held the lighter shook a little.

"Oh, it's dinner time," he said defeatedly, "and Jamie's feeling cantankerous." He gave her an embarrassed look. "I'm sorry, I'm sure you heard me yelling at him. He just won't fucking *eat*."

She reached over and rubbed his forearm lightly. The hairs on his bare arm were soft and velvety. "Can I help? Maybe he'll eat something if I sit with him. You know, the novelty."

"If you could get him to eat the lamb chop at least," Tom sighed, "I would kiss you a thousand times."

Teresa's eyes dropped and she felt her face warm. When she glanced up, she was suddenly very conscious of Tom's lips.

"That's quite an offer," she smiled and turned quickly to go to Jamie, who was already calling to her from the other room.

. . .

AFTER JAMIE died, Tom's friend Asher brought him one of his pet turtles named Endymion. It fit snugly in the palm of his hand, like a large avocado pit, and had beady, imploring eyes.

"I thought Tom could use some company," Asher explained to Teresa the day he presented Endymion in his kidney-shaped pool. "Someone to take care of. Turtles are the symbol of self-nurturing, you know."

Since Tom had been taking care of Jamie for the last few years, Teresa thought he didn't really need a new charge, and she said that after Asher had left.

"Asher means well," Tom defended. "He just loves turtles. He has something like ten of them. There are really big ones that have full reign of the house. They even watch TV. I'm just glad he didn't bring one of *those*."

Endymion was a fussy eater. "He needs a freshly killed goldfish every morning," Asher instructed.

"Great!" Teresa said to Tom. "Just what you need." But conscientiously each day, Tom stopped at the neighborhood pet shop on his way home from his morning walk through Central Park. He bought a live goldfish and carried it back in a plastic bag of water. He didn't want to buy them more than one at a time, for fear of them becoming pets rather than food. After he did this three days in a row, he explained his mission to the curious pet shop owner, who then began to have the fish waiting in its bag at nine o'clock sharp.

Endymion wouldn't eat the fish live, and he sat staring at them in confusion if their heads weren't cut off. So every morning Tom decapitated a small goldfish with a paring knife on the kitchen counter and laid it in the pool of water.

"I can't believe you do that," Teresa said in disgust. "I can't believe you pamper this turtle like that. What would it do in the wild? It would have to eat its fish whole, heads and all."

"I know," Tom sighed.

"I think," Teresa said, "Asher gave you this turtle because he was sick of lopping off goldfish heads."

"It's actually not so bad," Tom said. "You get used to it."

After all of Jamie's drug combinations, repeated infections, near blindness at the end, and countless stays in the hospital, Teresa reasoned that turtle feeding must seem minor.

In his second month with Tom, Endymion became unaccountably listless. His appetite dwindled to half a fish a day, and Tom had to scoop the uneaten half from the water. Tom asked the pet shop owner's advice, and she suggested some turtle vitamins. But soon Endymion could only sit on the upper deck of his pool, staring wearily at the goldfish. By the end of a week of not eating, he was belly up in the water.

"I seem to have killed Endymion," Tom said resignedly to Teresa on the phone. "Can you come up?"

An hour later she arrived and found that Tom hadn't touched the corpse. She lifted it gingerly from the water, deposited it in a plastic sack from Food Emporium and carried it carefully to one of the trash cans on the street. Its shell hit the bottom of the empty can with a sickening thud that made Teresa shiver.

"So long, Endymion," she said, because it seemed like she should say something.

Back in the apartment, she washed her hands and joined Tom in the living room. He was sitting with a vague look on his face, his hands folded neatly in his lap.

"What are you doing Saturday?" he asked.

She thought a moment, but only for effect. Her weekends were routinely open. "What did you have in mind?"

"A trip up Route 17," he said, and his eyes clouded.

"Okay," she replied.

. . .

GLORIA WAS sitting on the front stoop when Teresa got home. Teresa spotted her from the corner of Eighth Avenue but couldn't quite believe it.

"How long have you been here?" Teresa asked in surprise, plopping down next to her on the hot cement. The sun had just disappeared, leaving the late summer sky a magnificent wash of purples and roses.

"Not long," Gloria said, closing the book she was reading, a new Ruth Rendell mystery. "A couple of minutes. I called Tom's looking for you, but you'd just left, so I calculated how long it would take you on the train, and here I am."

Teresa stared past her at the sunset. "Seems like a lot of trouble," she observed. She was embarrassed that she hadn't returned five or six messages from Gloria on her answering machine, each one a little more impatient than the last. After the third one, Teresa felt she couldn't possibly face Gloria's anger.

"It's been a long time since you've returned phone calls," Gloria pointed out, "and I'm persistent."

Teresa cleared her throat but couldn't think of anything to say. "Sorry," she muttered sheepishly.

Gloria shook her head. "You're a piece of work," she said, but didn't elaborate. "You been at Tom's a lot, or just not answering the phone?"

"Both," Teresa admitted. "Tonight his turtle died, and he couldn't deal."

Gloria nodded. "Tom's a good guy."

"One of the best." Teresa glanced at her friend and noticed the little beads of sweat on her forehead, just below the hairline.

"Though I've been wondering why you seem to like him now more than, oh, your other friends," Gloria added, nervously riffling the pages of her book. "I mean, I understood you were busy when Jamie was sick, but it's been, what, a while now."

"Yeah, it's been a while," Teresa agreed vaguely, though she could have recited the exact number of months, weeks, and days since Jamie had died. She didn't appreciate the scolding; she didn't feel like she could hold her own in this argument. She didn't know why she needed Tom or he needed her, but the fact was they did. Why couldn't Gloria just see that?

"You cut me out," Gloria said sadly. She turned to Teresa with a questioning look. "Do you think I don't know anything about losing people? Do you think I haven't watched friends die of AIDS? Do you . . . " But she broke off abruptly just as her voice rose to an angry pitch. "Sometimes I want to shake you, you make me so mad. I want to say, who the fuck do you think you are to cut me out?" Gloria turned her head away and began slapping her paperback novel against the stoop.

"It isn't about *you*," Teresa said, softly laying a hand on Gloria's arm to still the repetitious sound of the book against cement. "I didn't decide to cut *you* out."

"Like hell," Gloria said hotly. "What, I'm supposed to say it's okay because you've cut out everyone? Everyone but Tom, that is." The last words had the bite of jealousy. "You made a decision, girlfriend, no matter what you want to believe."

Teresa stared at the book in Gloria's hands. When had she last read something for pleasure? She hadn't touched a book since she stopped reading the classics to Jamie months before. She used to always have a book on the subway. Now on the long ride to and from Tom's she simply read the overhead advertisements for roach control and cheap gynecological clinics, or watched other people in the car. She and Gloria had often shared books, turning them over to each other with capsulized reviews.

"Not one of her best, but *great* sex."

"This is the first mystery in a long time where I didn't guess the killer on page twenty."

"Are you even listening to me?" Gloria was asking angrily, and Teresa nodded unconvincingly. She almost said, "I'd rather not talk about it," but had the unexpected, alarming feeling that that's what her own mother might say.

"You are a piece of work," Gloria repeated, standing up and shoving the paperback into the back pocket of her cutoffs. "And why I hauled my ass over here I'll never know." The cement had creased little bumps into the backs of Gloria's thighs. Impulsively, Teresa grabbed one of her ankles.

"I didn't have much for dinner," she smiled up at her friend. "Just some salad. Want to split a pizza?"

Gloria yanked herself free and sat back down on the stoop with a sigh. "Only if it's with pepperoni," she conceded. "And only if you pay."

. . .

SPANKY AND Lulu were their first and only pets. Their mother didn't like having animals in the house but consented to the two goldfish Alison won at St. Sebastian's annual bazaar, even though she said they wouldn't live long without a proper tank.

"You two have to take care of them," their mother warned. "You feed them and change their water. But I'll tell you again, they won't live long."

Their father thought from their coloring that they were both male, but Alison decided they were a couple. "I want to call them Spanky and Lulu," she announced, and Teresa agreed because Alison had won them after all.

They went to the pet department of Kresge's 5&10 with their father and bought a bowl, pink gravel, a ceramic castle, and some seaweed. They also got a pamphlet titled "Caring for Your Goldfish," but it emphasized the need for a tank and filter, which their father priced and rejected with a stern shake of his head.

"You'll have them a week or two at most," he noted. "They're very fragile."

Every morning it was Alison's turn to sprinkle food into the bowl, and every afternoon it was Teresa's.

"I think you feed them too much," their mother observed, but Alison disagreed.

"They look a little scrawny," she said, and Teresa concurred.

"Yeah, Spanky's *real* little," Teresa said, dumping in a few more flakes. "He needs to grow."

Within a week, Lulu had taken to hovering behind one of the castle towers. Spanky rested his now fat belly along the pink gravel. When Alison tapped the glass to get their attention, they didn't budge, except to bob in the current of water her tapping made.

"They're sick," Alison commented sadly. "Maybe they need more food." She littered the water with flakes, but neither fish made a move to touch them. The next morning, their orange bodies floated on the surface among the flakes. Lulu's nestled between the twin towers.

"They're gone, girls," their mother said. "You overfed them. I warned you. Now we have to flush them down the toilet."

"No!" Alison screamed, and Teresa stared wide-eyed at her sister.

"All right, all right," their mother gave in quickly, and she searched the closet in vain for a small box to bury them in. Finally Alison emptied her sixteen-count Crayola crayon box and offered that up for her pets.

They buried them with a garden trowel in the brick planter in the back yard, among their mother's carefully tended geraniums. Alison stuck a cross made from popsicle sticks in the ground with "Spanky and Lulu Keenan" written on it in colored pencil. The next heavy rainstorm destroyed the marker, but Alison remembered the spot anyway. Every now and then she said to Teresa, "Remember Spanky and Lulu? I miss them, don't you?"

. . .

THEY DROVE in comfortable silence. Tom had become so familiar to her he was like a hand or foot she couldn't imagine being without. Occasionally they turned to each other and smiled. Tom glanced into the rearview mirror at the canister and book on the back seat.

At Pal's they ordered blueberry pancakes and smothered them in butter and maple syrup. Teresa couldn't finish hers, so Tom did. Afterwards he sat and rubbed his full stomach. They idled over coffee that was so strong it made Teresa's hand shake after just one cup.

"I finished my novel," she announced proudly, though she knew he hadn't progressed far with his and hoped her achievement wouldn't discourage him.

Tom tapped his juice glass to hers. "Congratulations," he beamed. "That's terrific."

"It's dedicated to Jamie," she added, cautiously. Would he be sad that she'd beaten him to the punch?

Tom finished his coffee. "I'm sure it's fabulous. *You're* fabulous. I'd really like to read it," he said earnestly.

She smiled again at his uncomplicated love. What had made her think she would lose him after Jamie? Yet, he was only fifty, an attractive widower who would undoubtedly find another man, as she would eventually let herself go to another woman. Their closeness now was a bridge between two places.

"I love you," she said, well aware that she had never said that to anyone but lovers and Jamie. Love was such a distant emotion. Her mother found verbalizing it unnecessary, her father never said much of anything. Then the first time Dana whispered "I love you" in her ear as her body shook on top of hers, the sound of it so startled Teresa she couldn't come, no matter how hard she concentrated.

"It's entirely mutual," Tom smiled back.

In the diner parking lot, Tom unscrewed the lid of the canister and handed it to Teresa with the book of poems. She stared in at the ashes, a coarse white reminiscent of gravel.

"Do you mind doing it?" he asked, and she shook her head.

They drove off down Route 17 and at some point Tom simply said, "Now's good."

She held the canister out the window with both hands and watched the ashes fly back into the wind. It reminded her of times she'd seen Jamie empty his car ashtray. She rolled the window up and said nervously, "I hope we don't get stopped for littering. Wouldn't Jamie love *that!*"

"I was watching for cops," Tom replied seriously.

She opened the book of Whitman poems in her lap to the marked page and read aloud slowly.

At the last, tenderly,
From the walls of the powerful fortress'd house,
From the clasp of the knitted locks, from the keep of the
*   well-closed doors,*
Let me be wafted.
Let me glide noiselessly forth;
With the key of softness unlock the locks—with a whis-
*   per,*
Set ope the doors O soul.
Tenderly—be not impatient,
(Strong is your hold O mortal flesh,
Strong is your hold O love.)

The book closed quietly, and she glimpsed over at Tom, whose eyelashes were wet. She had never seen him cry, not when Jamie died, not at the memorial. He must do it, she thought, alone at night. She refused to believe he didn't cry at all.

"You read very well," was all he said, and by then his eyes were dry.

. . .

HER FATHER left early in the morning for his flight back to Pittsburgh, and, at his insistence, Teresa did not accompany him to the airport. "I don't want to be a bother," he said. "I'm sure you have a lot to do." At the door of her apartment, she hugged him, his body stiff and awkward in her embrace.

"You remember what you promised?" he asked. "That you wouldn't mention our talk last night to your mother?"

"Yes," Teresa said, already annoyed at herself for colluding with her father once more. Teresa watched from the window of her apartment as he hailed and entered a cab, considering as she did how the two of them had been complacent partners in the gag order in their family. Neither had pushed her mother to acknowledge her own grief and theirs, to let the family try to find a new, though forever altered, life. She and her parents had been residents of the same house, they ate together, exchanged presents at Christmas. Their dirty clothes had all ended up in the same laundry basket. But Teresa remembered something different, a feeling of lives bound up together in a bigger way. It was a vague memory, but it tugged at her just the same. They survived Alison's death in different ways: Teresa ran away, her father retreated further inward, her mother denied. But surviving wasn't the same as mending. And mending, she thought, had nothing to do with forgetting and everything to do with memory.

Teresa cleared a space from her desk where she had been working on her novel. Since Jamie's death, the words had inexplicably come more easily, passing effortlessly through her fingers to the computer keys. There was almost too much to say, too little space to say it in. How could she contain her thoughts in a single book, a mere two or three hundred pages?

She found a sheet of paper and a felt-tip pen and wrote the date across the top of the page. "Dear Mom," she started and stopped, contemplating her father's request of silence. The apartment suddenly felt smaller than ever, contracting on all sides. She grabbed a pen and a notebook and took her letter into the street.

Teresa walked to the Bleecker Street playground, which was already alive with parents and children. She found an unoccupied bench and sat and observed the action around her. A toddler wearing bright yellow plastic roller skates was being led by her mother's hand across the cement. A stone caught her wheel, and her mother rescued her just before she hit the ground with a cry.

"Dad asked me not to say anything," Teresa wrote, "but I'm breaking my promise to him."

Two little boys ran breathlessly into her bench and froze, waiting for her reproach. But Teresa just smiled and said hi, and they ran laughing in the opposite direction.

"I was stunned to find out you'd had a miscarriage before Alison, but it helped me understand more clearly what you must have gone through when Alison died."

A father and daughter sat down at the other end of the bench, making Teresa's notebook jiggle and the word "died" squiggle under her pen. The father began reading aloud to the little girl from *Eloise*.

"I think I understand, too, why you just wanted to try to put it behind you, but I'm not sure that's been the best thing for any of us. I wish we could sit down some time and talk about what that was like for all of us, losing a sister and daughter with so much vitality that it seemed like her death drained the life from all of us."

Teresa's visual memory of Alison had blurred over time, as had her own image of herself as a child. She closed her eyes tightly, half-listening to the familiar story of Eloise, the little girl who lived at the Plaza Hotel, and half-trying to conjure up a picture.

They had looked alike, everyone said so. In studio photos of them when they were small, the main characteristic that distinguished them was that Alison's head reached slightly above Teresa's. Teresa wondered suddenly if that, too, had contributed to her mother's despair, the realization that every time she looked at Teresa she would also see the daughter she lost. There had been many times when Teresa had felt the absence of her mother's regard, as if she were looking through her rather than at her, or just beyond her to something over her head. Teresa had always assumed it was about her, something bad she had done to displease her mother.

She capped her pen when the little girl on yellow roller skates rolled into her accidentally, leaving a thin gash of black ink across the letter. It didn't matter. Teresa couldn't send it anyway, not yet. When it was time, she'd write it over, neatly, on stationery she bought specially for the occasion.

. . .

TWO EVENINGS in a row she spoke to his answering machine instead of him. "Tom, you popular boy," she teased the machine on the second evening, "where *are* you?"

It was unlike him not to return calls, but for that matter, it was unlike him to be out all evening. After the second try, she replaced the receiver with a queasy feeling. She pictured him lying on the living room floor, unable to get to the phone, arm weakly outstretched to it. She still had his apartment keys and wondered about using them unannounced. In two days, a person could die, she thought, as she redialed the familiar number.

"Tom," she said, hearing her own voice shake, "please

call me. I'm worried. Where *are* you?"

That night, when he didn't call, she had a nightmare. In it Robin was dead, and no one told Teresa. Robin was accidentally knocked down by her girlfriend, hit her head on something sharp and died. Teresa woke sitting upright, staring out the bedroom window, disoriented and scared.

Finally, Tom called her in the morning at work. She was drinking coffee and wondering if she should try him at the TV studio.

"Teresa," he said, "it's Tom."

"I know," she said. "Don't you think I know your voice by now? You're all right then."

"I'm sorry you worried," he replied, a non-answer. "You shouldn't."

She bit a nail, wondering why he didn't offer more, wondering how she could ask. "Well, two days. *You* know."

He said nothing, then sighed. "Well, I know you'll disapprove, but I sort of had a date. I mean, I *had* a date. I wanted to try it out."

"For two days?" she snapped, then relented. "I'm sorry. It's none of my business."

"Obviously, it *is* your business somehow or I wouldn't tell you," he said, sounding both impatient and confused at why it *was* her business. "You know, Teresa, it's been a really long time since I had sex."

She softened at his plaintive tone. "Who is he?" she asked, imagining a young stud with classic good looks, broad shoulders, full lips. Tom's type, or what she assumed would be his type.

"No one you know," he answered vaguely. "Asher fixed us up. It was a blind date."

"Asher," she repeated, chuckling. "I thought his specialty was turtles."

Tom laughed, "Yeah, well, he's a little better at picking out men than pets."

She pictured Tom at his office desk, feet up, smoking, staring at his computer screen, tapping a pen, nervous about having to confess. Why did it matter so much? Because nothing had changed but at the same time virtually everything had. "So he's a hump?" she managed to ask, trying to lighten up and put him more at ease.

He laughed again, bigger, more self-assured. "Yeah, he's a hump."

"Does this hump have a name?"

"Will," he said, sighing or exhaling smoke, she couldn't tell. "His name's Will."

She sighed then, too. "Are you going to see him again?"

The pause was so extended, she asked if he was still on the line. "Yes, of course I'm still here," he replied. "You know, Teresa, I like Will a lot. He's not Jamie, but he's a grownup. I *would* like to see him again, but . . ."

"But?"

"We practiced safe sex, but if I start *seeing* someone, I feel like I should probably be tested."

"That would make sense," she said, relief flooding her heart. She wasn't sure why it was important for her to know Tom's sero-status, but it was. She thought it had something to do with being prepared.

"Sense," he said with a wry laugh. "My darling, nothing's made *sense* to me for a long time."

.   .   .

THE RAINBOW Room was just as she expected, a slice of the big band era poised at the top of Manhattan. Tom had wanted someplace less "touristy," like Cafe des Artistes, but Jamie had insisted on being able to dance. Their extravagance embarrassed Teresa and thrilled her at the same time. She had never spent more for dinner than twenty dollars, but Tom and Jamie were prepared to spend many times that amount.

"Here we go," Jamie smiled, as the waiter brought their champagne. They sat in the dining tier beyond the dance floor, watching heterosexual couples swirl across the floor to band music Teresa recognized from her parents' record collection. Teresa wore her only dress, a calf-length, liquid blue rayon that looked much more expensive than its thirty-five-dollar price tag. She bought it at an Indian bazaar on Eighth Street that was perpetually going out of business but never did. She had even shaved her legs for the occasion, though her razor had bitten her several times, and her smoky stockings hid the nicks.

The waiter filled their champagne flutes and set the bottle in its silver-plated bucket beside the table. Jamie cleared his throat and inclined his glass toward the center of the table.

"To my niece, the novelist," he said with pride. "Here's to big sales and rave reviews of your first book!"

"Here here," Tom added, and they clinked their glasses, sounding a delightful musical peal.

"It's a small press, you know," Teresa said, after her first sip, the urge to downplay her own success overcoming her, "not the big time." Her mother's words when she announced her accomplishment still echoed in her ears.

"Is that what they call a vanity press?" her mother had asked, naively but hurtfully just the same, as if she couldn't imagine what real publisher would want Teresa's work.

"Artemis Press is great," Tom pointed out. "I love their stuff. It's a wonderful achievement, and you shouldn't belittle it. You sound like your mother."

"Did you ever think when you were scratching your stories into notebooks when you were a kid that this would happen some day?" Jamie asked.

"Well," Teresa said, "you know, I never really thought about it. It was kind of a game, you know, like other kids play tag or kickball. It's just how I kept myself busy, how I got over missing Alison."

She remembered clearly all the times she had sat hunched over her desk in her bedroom, writing longhand into spiral notebooks from Woolworth's and Kresge's, while the diffuse sounds of children at play in the street drifted through the window. Instead of candy bars or chewing gum at the supermarket, she begged her mother to buy her tablets of paper. Her mother groused a few times—"Do you have to use the paper up so quickly?"—but more often than not gave in to the request, because she knew it occupied Teresa in her room for hours on end. "It keeps her busy," Teresa heard her mother tell Mrs. DeNardo. "Better that she's inside where I can keep my eye on her, than running around the street with the other kids, being hit by a car or getting into who knows what trouble!"

Jamie ordered caviar, which she had never tasted before, and the delicate roe popped sensuously under her teeth. "You're spending more on dinner than I'll ever make on this book!" Teresa quipped.

"This is just the start of your career," Jamie noted. "Someday, it's a Pulitzer for you!"

"And the National Book Award," Tom chimed in.

"Hell, why not the Nobel Prize?" Jamie smiled, fluttering his cracker excitedly in the air and losing a few dots of caviar.

"Now let's talk about your book party," Tom suggested. "We can have it at our house. How many people do you want to invite?"

"Really, you guys are going too far," Teresa objected. "No party. This dinner is more than I ever expected."

"That's why we're doing it," Jamie said, "because you never expect anything. Time to start thinking big, Teresa. Time to start expecting more from life. Tom and I won't always be around to make sure you do."

He was right, she had never counted on much for herself. So much of her early identity had been as Alison's "little sister." Then, on paper, Carla Carlotta had lived for her. As a teenager bound for college, she'd relegated her small lifetime of writing to an unmarked box that vanished in her parents' house. As an adult, she still referred to her writing as a hobby and never tried to publish even one story. She misplaced pieces she was working on, threw others that displeased her away without looking back. The novel had happened by accident, a story that kept growing until it burst the page limits she set for her writing. When she'd finished the novel, the first major writing project she'd accomplished since childhood, Jamie suggested she send it to a publisher, and she had laughed and called him crazy. But the more she contemplated it, the more it seemed like a possibility, the more it seemed like what she wanted for herself—an identity of her own, a validation of herself in the world, a knowledge of Teresa Keenan—and the more it seemed like she'd wasted a lot of years not taking herself or her writing seriously.

When her advance copy of the book arrived in the mail, she held it close for a long time, her hands stroking the smooth cover, her finger skimming her name on the spine. She had called it *Almost There* because that seemed like her own location in life—on her way, but not quite to her destination. What was her destination, anyway? She had no real idea. But she was off and running, counting on Jamie to sprint along at her side as her coach.

Between the main course and dessert, Jamie squired her across the dance floor while Tom watched from the table, enjoying a cigarette with the last of the champagne. She was not used to dancing with a man, and she followed his steps with trepidation, her inclination to stare at her feet winning out several times. Was everyone watching her stumble over her uncle's feet? He spoke to her with ardent encouragement, an intimate voice in her ear. "You're doing fine, sweetie," he said kindly. "Just let yourself go."

Through the windows of the Rainbow Room, the lights of Manhattan sparkled like a handful of glitter tossed into the sky. She clasped Jamie's arm more tightly and recalled the few times she had danced on his feet as a little girl, her patent leather Mary Janes atop his expansive cordovan Oxfords. When she was small, she had squealed with delight as he spun her around her parents' living room, humming melodies she didn't recognize. But now, in another time and city, another life almost, she simply and quietly savored the clean scent of his after-shave, the warm moistness of his hand around hers.

. . .

"THIS WILL be good for you," Gloria said firmly. "You need to get out in the world again, girlfriend. Tom's found someone, why shouldn't you?"

Gloria, who was herself looking for someone to date, had coaxed Teresa to a women's dance at the Community Center. Teresa had relented after much pressure, though she insisted on being able to leave whenever she wanted to.

"No one's got handcuffs on you," Gloria teased, her eyes wandering the vast expanse of the auditorium. "Lighten up."

It looked vaguely like a high school dance, only without the boys. The organizers had decked pink and lavender streamers across the ceiling. A DJ was seated on a makeshift platform above the dance floor, blasting an appealing salsa rhythm, and women crammed the space in twos and threes that blended into one mass of bodies.

"Look, there's Marta," Gloria said, pointing toward a tall redhead who blew her a kiss and waved to them to join her. "Let's dance!"

Teresa hesitated and remained firmly in place on the sidelines. "You go ahead, I'll watch for a while," she said, tapping her foot to the beat in spite of herself. It was stuffy in the room and she used the temperature as an excuse. "It's hot. I need something to drink first, then I'll come dance."

Gloria raised a suspicious eyebrow. "Promise?"

"Cross my heart," she smiled.

Teresa watched as Gloria bounced into the middle of the crowd, hugging Marta and her girlfriend. Gloria was admirably unself-conscious about her dancing and moved comfortably with the music. Teresa still often watched her feet when she danced and held her arms stiffly at her sides.

"Loosen up!" Gloria was always saying when they danced together, taking hold of Teresa's arms and waving them about. "Let it go!"

Teresa wandered to the bar and tried to order a seltzer and cranberry juice, but a volunteer bartender told her she needed a drink ticket first. The ticket table was at the opposite end of the dance floor, and as Teresa approached it, she broke into a nervous sweat.

"Teresa!"

It was too late to turn away; she'd been spotted by the woman selling drink tickets. She held out five dollars.

"Day," she said, trying to be cool and calm. "How are you?"

"Good, good," Day said, accidentally ripping a ticket in half and laughing nervously. "You... I was hoping I would see you again. When a friend of mine asked me to help out here tonight, I wondered if this was the sort of thing you'd come to, but I didn't think so."

"I wouldn't have come on my own, but my friend Gloria dragged me out," Teresa said. Then, after a pause, "Look, I'm sorry I didn't call, I..."

"It's okay, really," Day said, shaking her head a little too vigorously. "I understand. Life."

Teresa accepted five tickets from her with a puzzled look.

She had really only wanted two, but hadn't made that clear. "Life?" she asked.

"Yeah, life is almost too much sometimes."

"Oh, yeah," Teresa smiled. "Life."

A small line of women had formed behind Teresa, and she stepped aside to let them buy their tickets. Day ignored her until there was a break in the line.

"Maybe we . . . maybe I could call *you*," Day suggested casually.

"Sure," Teresa said, twisting her tickets in her hand. "I mean, sure, why don't you?" She smiled and begged out of the awkward conversation. "I've got to find Gloria before she thinks I bolted. It's great to see you."

"Enjoy yourself. Don't spend all those tickets in one place," Day said with a flirtatious grin. Teresa blushed, suddenly remembering that she'd had fun before flirting with Day. She waved at her and went back to the bar.

"Where'd you disappear to?" Gloria said, coming up behind her and taking her arm. "You promised you'd dance!"

"Okay, okay," Teresa said, giving in to her friend's insistence and letting herself be pulled onto the dance floor. The DJ had switched to early eighties disco music, and Gloria squealed with delight.

"Yow! It's my song!" she yelped, as the intro to "Gloria" started up. She raised her hands over her head and jumped vigorously to the music. "Come on, girlfriend!"

Slowly, cautiously, Teresa's arms went into the air. She twisted and churned and mimicked her friend's movements. All of a sudden, she was dancing.

.   .   .

SHE FOUND the old projector in the back of her closet, hovering against the wall. The movies took longer to locate. Two of them were hiding in the far corner of a desk drawer, gathering pencil shavings. The rest were in a box under the bed labeled in Jamie's printing, "Misc. Chatchkas," mixed in with seashells, ceramic knickknacks she'd gotten as gifts, envelopes of snapshots she hadn't looked at in years.

"There's some white wine in the refrigerator," she called to Day, who had never been to her apartment. "On the second shelf. There's a corkscrew in the far right drawer. Somewhere. If you can't find it, holler." *Stop babbling*, she thought, *it's unbecoming.*

Day relaxed and made herself at home, opening drawers and cupboards. She uncorked the wine and poured a big glass for each of them while Teresa set up the equipment to project onto the wall over the sofa bed, the only big, blank space in the apartment.

"I haven't seen a projector like that in twenty years," Day laughed at the cumbersome machine.

"That's about how old it is," Teresa said. She fumbled with switches and knobs, trying to remember what operated what. "In its day this was quite a piece of equipment."

Liane bought it at a discount camera store in midtown Manhattan, where the Hasidic salesmen in yarmulkahs and white shirts buttoned to the neck stared suspiciously at the girl with a star painted on her cheek as she waved plastic in the air. "I want the best," Liane announced. "Compliments of Harry Levin." What had Liane's father said when she left the projector at Fordham for Teresa?

Day reclined on the rug next to Teresa and her projector.

"Now what would you care to view first, madame—*Teresa Tarts It Up* or *Teresa Times Two?*" Teresa asked with a grin.

"Oh, definitely *Teresa Tarts It Up*," Day replied huskily.

On the bare white wall, Teresa cavorted in tight purple hotpants that made her wince. "My God," she groaned, "look at those thighs! I was living on buttered popcorn and canned frosting. No wonder Liane never made a pass at me."

"You look good," Day contradicted. "You have a nice butt."

Teresa blushed at the present tense of Day's comment. "We were so silly," she said, embarrassed. "I can't believe how young I was."

The next reel was a short that Teresa had filmed, an extended and shaky shot of Liane smoking a cigarette, luxuriously and sensuously. She caressed the cigarette with her lips like a lover's private parts.

"So your first love was a hippie," Day remarked, noting the little star painted on Liane's cheek. It was a black outline filled in with metallic silver.

"Sort of, I guess," Teresa agreed. "A free spirit, at any rate."

"What happened to her?"

The film flapped off the reel noisily. "I don't know," Teresa said. "I never saw her again." The hum of the projector's fan filled in the gaps in the conversation. "More? Or have you had enough?"

"More," Day said, refilling both their wine glasses. Teresa was already feeling a warm buzz.

The next movie was *Teresa Times Two*. For close to three minutes, Teresa stared out at them with different expressions from a reflection in her dorm room mirror. At the end, she turned and faced the camera, her eyes large and eerily light. She put a hand to her mouth and blew a kiss to Liane, the camera woman, and to the audience.

"Well," Teresa said self-consciously, "maybe that's enough memory lane stuff."

As she rewound the film, Teresa thought about another movie she had, the one her father had sent her when he returned to Pittsburgh after Jamie's memorial. It came in a small box addressed to "Ms. Teresa Keenan," and she had guessed it was the home movie of her and Alison at Lake Erie without even reading his note.

"Dear Teresa," her father wrote, "I thought you'd like to have this. You'll watch it more than I can. You and Alison were so little! It's hard to remember you being this small, not even knowing how to swim yet. Take care of yourself. Here's a little something for the food I ate at your house." A ten-dollar bill lay on top of the movie, and Teresa smiled at it. She imagined her father sitting alone in the living room while her mother was out of the house, at church maybe. Teresa pictured him playing the movie one last time, then tucking a bill from his wallet into the package before he mailed it off to her. Teresa considered sharing the movie with Day, but she decided it was too soon to bring up Alison. She hadn't even worked up to talking about Jamie yet, but there was time for that.

She let the projector cool down, and Day remained quiet, finishing her wine. Though they hardly knew each other, it was not an awkward silence. Later, in bed, Teresa didn't cry.

Paula Martinac is a writer, editor and activist. Her first novel, *Out of Time* (Seal, 1990), won the 1990 Lambda Literary Award for Lesbian Fiction. Her short stories were featured in *Voyages Out 1* (Seal, 1989) and have appeared in numerous journals and anthologies. A former editor of *Conditions* magazine, she also edited the anthology *The One You Call Sister: New Women's Fiction* (Cleis, 1989). Born and raised in Pittsburgh, she lives in New York City, where she is working on a third novel.

Selected Titles from Seal Press

OUT OF TIME by Paula Martinac. $9.95, 0-931188-91-1. Winner of the 1990 Lambda Literary Award for Best Lesbian Fiction, *Out of Time* is a delightful and thoughtful novel about lesbian history and the power of memory.

ALMA ROSE by Edith Forbes. $10.95, 1-878067-33-8. A brilliant novel filled with unforgettable characters and the vibrant spirit of the West, *Alma Rose* is a warm, funny and endearing tale of life and love off the beaten track, by a gifted lesbian writer.

MARGINS by Terri de la Peña. $10.95, 1-878067-19-2. One of the first lesbian novels by a Chicana author, *Margins* is an insightful story about family relationships, recovery from loss, creativity and love.

GIRLS, VISIONS AND EVERYTHING by Sara Schulman. $9.95, 0-931188-38-5. A spirited romp through Manhatten's Lower East Side featuring lesbian-at-large Lila Futuransky. By the author of *People in Trouble*, *After Delores* and *Empathy*.

ANOTHER AMERICA by Barbara Kingsolver. $10.95, Paper, 1-878067-15-X. $14.95, Cloth, 1-878067-14-1. A stunning first collection of poetry by the bestselling author of *Animal Dreams* and *The Bean Trees*.

THE FORBIDDEN POEMS by Becky Birtha. $10.95, 1-878067-01-X. Chronicling a journey of loss and mending, this provocative first collection of poetry exhibits a strength of vision and richness of language by a noted African-American lesbian writer.

LESBIAN COUPLES; *Creating Healthy Relationships for the 90s* by D. Merilee Clunis and G. Dorsey Green. $12.95, 1-878067-37-0. A new edition of the highly acclaimed and popular guide for lesbians in couple relationships.

SEAL PRESS, founded in 1976 to provide a forum for women writers and feminist issues, has many other titles in stock: fiction, self-help books, anthologies and international literature. Any of the books above may be ordered from us at 3131 Western Ave., Suite 410, Seattle WA 98121 (please include 15% of total book order for shipping and handling). Write us for a free catalog or if you would like to be on our mailing list.